ALWAYS TOMORROW

Jim Perry

Always Tomorrow
Copyright © 2024 by Jim Perry

Library of Congress Control Number: 2024902611
ISBN-13:   Paperback: 978-1-64749-942-6
            Hardback: 978-1-64749-976-1
            Epub: 978-1-64749-943-3

Printed in the United States of America

GoToPublish LLC
1-888-337-1724
www.gotopublish.com
info@gotopublish.com

CONTENTS

Dedication...v
Chapter 1.. 1
Chapter 2.. 19
Chapter 3...37
Chapter 4 53
Chapter 5 65
Chapter 6 71
Chapter 7.. 81
Chapter 8 93
Chapter 9 103
Chapter 10...115
Chapter 11 125
Chapter 12 133
Epilogue 145

DEDICATION

This book is dedicated to my beloved wife, Kay. I was blessed to share twenty-nine years and eight months with her love, support, and faith in God. She encouraged me in all my endeavors, including this book. She helped me see that all things are possible and that, with perseverance, dedication, and truth, great things can be achieved. I look forward to the day I hold her once again, to be able to spend eternity expressing my gratitude for her as we walk together forever.

ALWAYS TOMORROW

CHAPTER 1

....

L eaving the busy airport behind, the bus maneuvered through heavy afternoon traffic. As the bus finally turned onto the highway, heading south, the traffic seemed to thin out a bit, with every driver vying for a spot at the front of the small group of automobiles that whizzed by. Soon, the nearly empty bus gained enough speed to flow smoothly down the right side of three lanes, allowing the impatient afternoon commuters free rein to dodge one another, always seeming to want to get in front of the next vehicle they encountered.

The airport had not been particularly busy. It was a Tuesday, and most commuters traveled on the weekends. In the terminal, there were only a couple of Vietnam War protesters who gave him a scowl as he walked by but made no threatening moves toward him. He was required to travel in uniform, which made him somewhat a target of those opposing the war. He paid little attention to them as he passed, though they clearly recognized him as another soldier taking part in what they saw as an unjust endeavor by the government. They had no idea, of course, that he was stationed in Europe as a mechanic and had no part in what they were protesting. Now, in 1971, the war seemed to be winding down, with more troops going to Western Europe than in 'Nam.

Sergeant Ben Dawson sat quietly near the back of the bus, gazing out the window and paying no attention to the speeding cars or the scenery that moved past in the afternoon sun. The pictures in his mind weren't in any way related to what the few other passengers were enjoying. Instead, he saw only a scrambled vision of the events of the last couple of days that changed everything he knew and looked forward to. Just hours ago, he learned he would be traveling home from his Germany duty station to bury his parents.

While he was still reeling from the news delivered to him by his Commander and First Sergeant, it all seemed like a bad dream, certainly a mistake. Maybe they had the wrong Dawson. There must be plenty of other Dawsons in the Army. And surely there was at least one or two in Germany. Unfortunately, that had been proven to not be the case. The Red Cross might make a mistake now and then, but this wasn't one of those times.

There were no details provided, only that his parents were deceased and he had to go home on emergency leave. With only an hour or so to pack and get to the airport, he didn't even have time to digest it all. It wasn't until he was on the flight out of Rhein-Main Airport that the reality began to settle in.

They were gone. Period. And with no siblings to help, it fell on him to make the arrangements and lay them to rest. The eleven-hour headache he endured had begun to fade now, replaced with what could only be described as a fog. Had they made arrangements for this already? He suspected so. His father was a highly organized and detail-oriented former intelligence officer, having served in the Army for over twenty-six years, retiring as a Brigadier General. With him, everything had a place, and everything had better be in it.

Who had to be notified? Ben knew a few of his family's friends, but not all. And what about an obituary? Everyone got one of those, didn't they? Who wrote it, and what did you do with it once it got done? Should they be separate, or one obituary for both of them? They were so close, after all.

As the Chesapeake Bay Bridge came into view, another sense of dread came over him. He always hated the bridge: it was high, long, and had a curve in it, not to mention, only one lane in each direction. As a result, automobiles came shockingly close to one another as they passed by. Cars were bad enough, but meeting a large truck usually took his breath away. He supposed that being afraid of heights didn't help much, so next to flying, this was almost like a phobia, and it seemed he would be getting a taste of both in one day.

To take his mind off things or to add to the stresses he already felt, he thought of Allie. She certainly didn't stress him, just the circumstances that pulled them so many miles apart the last few days. He met her one spring day, in the motor pool, of all places. She, too, was a soldier and worked as a mechanic in a support unit that handled upper-echelon maintenance for the three battalions on the small base. Since there were no barracks facilities on post and she was one of two female soldiers assigned to her unit, Ben was detailed by his commander to assist them in finding off-base housing. He could speak German pretty well, so they thought he might be of some help.

It didn't take long to get them an apartment and even less time for Ben to become smitten with her. In spite of her greasy coveralls and windblown hair, she was clearly the most beautiful woman he had ever seen. Soon they were dating, sightseeing, going to dinner, and otherwise spending a lot of off-duty time together. It seemed she felt the same way Ben did, but he wasn't certain.

Not long before Ben got the tragic news about his parents and was whisked back to the States, he decided to muster up the courage to tell her that he was, in fact, in love with her. Fear of rejection or that she didn't feel as strongly as he did had kept him from saying anything that might ruin their relationship. He figured he would go for the gusto and get it out there once and for all. After all, didn't she once ask him how to say "I love you" in German? He had joked about her having a German boyfriend, but the question stuck in his mind since then. Maybe she was just fishing, trying to figure out a way to say it without really saying it.

When he left on emergency leave, she was on a training exercise somewhere in central Germany. Her unit was supporting some other units, and she was obligated to go. Due back to base in a couple of weeks, he would tell her then and not let the chance slip away. And he wouldn't have much time as she was finishing up her enlistment and would be processing out of the Army soon after her return. After that, she would be thousands of miles away in her home in Albuquerque, New Mexico. Though not a pleasant thought, at least he would be able to find her, and they could possibly get on with their life together. The problem now was that he had no detailed information on exactly where in Albuquerque she lived, no phone number or anything that would lead him to her. Knowing more about that detail of her life was something he could find out tomorrow. His only chance to save their relationship and their future together was to wrap things up here and get back to Germany as soon as he could.

Now, with something else to worry about, he could only sit back in his seat and close his eyes. The headache that had nearly faded was returning, maybe because of a lack of sleep or the fact he hadn't eaten in who knew how many hours. He decided it was best to just focus on the task at hand and concern himself with other matters after a good rest and a full stomach.

By now, the Bay Bridge was far behind, and home was mere minutes away. Though it had been a little over four years since he had seen the landscape that passed by, he had no interest in the familiar sights or any changes that may have taken place during his absence. All he wanted to do right now was see home again. Fully aware it wouldn't be the same, he felt it was still a place where he would be safe and reasonably comfortable, in spite of all that had happened.

As the bus crossed the Choptank River Bridge, Ben realized he had no transportation to his home in Church Creek, sixteen miles below Cambridge. He would likely call a cab to get the rest of the way home, where he had all the transportation he needed in the garage.

The bus made a right turn at the first intersection after the bridge, then a left at the first street. It slowed two blocks later and parked next to a small building that was the town's Greyhound terminal. The door opened before the wheels even stopped turning. Ben got up from his seat and slowly moved forward toward the open door, waiting until the other few passengers exited. Stepping down onto solid ground, the sun glaring down, he welcomed the warm spring breeze on his face. He noticed a couple of people glance at him with a smile, as if to welcome him home. Little did they know what lay before him in the next few weeks. Nevertheless, he smiled back and retrieved his bag from the bus storage bin and stepped into the shade of the generous awning of the terminal, glancing around for a phone. There was a phone booth at the rear corner of the building, and as he stepped toward it, he heard his name.

"That you, Ben?" came a voice from behind him.

As he turned around to find the source, he instantly recognized a familiar face.

"Jim. Jim Vickers. How are you? It's good to see you," Ben said, genuinely happy to see an old friend. Jim was a handsome young man, and his uniform fit him well. A little stocky, but Ben figured that was mostly muscle. His overall demeanor was one of confidence and authority, even for his young age.

"I'm doin' just fine, buddy. I heard you would be coming home soon," Jim said as he presented his hand for what turned out to be a hearty handshake.

"Guess you heard. And look at you. I knew you always wanted to get into law enforcement, but I thought you'd be a town cop. So what are you now? A sheriff?" Ben was clearly surprised.

Jim chuckled a bit and said, "The town cop job was too confining. I wanted to be able to get out, move around the county a bit. You meet more people that way, find out what's really going on around here. You know me. I was always a bit nosy, anyway. And look at you. Nice uniform, shiny brass, ribbons all over, gold rope thing hanging over your shoulder. And them shoes, shinier than mine. Looks like you've done well, even made Sergeant. Knew you would."

"And look at you. The county sheriff. A real police car and everything, not like when you cruised around town in your daddy's Buick, wearing that cowboy hat. You could clear a parking lot pretty quick till everybody figured out who you were. Guess now you're official," Ben said.

"Yep, and guess what, I'm still wearing that same hat, 'cept now I have more trouble clearing these kids from the parking lots than when I was only playin' the part." He laughed. "But they don't cause us any trouble, just get a little loud now and then, especially over at the Tasty Freeze on Saturday nights. But the town cops deal with that. I usually just sit and watch if I'm in town. Anyway, we can catch up later. Throw your bag in the back, and I'll run you down home. I'm sure you could use rest 'bout now."

"Yes. Yes, I could. And thanks, but aren't you on duty?" Ben asked.

"Yep," Jim said with a grin. "But part of my duty is patrol, and that's what I'll be doin': patrollin' from here to Church Creek. Now get in before I have to cuff ya."

"Should I sit in the back and look sad?" Ben asked with a smile.

"No, that'll just get the town talkin' more than they already do. Wouldn't look good, a soldier as a prisoner soon as he gets into town."

"Thanks, Jim. For just a couple minutes, I almost forgot why I came home," Ben said, as his smile slowly faded.

"I'll be here for ya, buddy, and so will the rest of the guys," Jim said that with sincerity, and Ben knew it.

The few people at the bus station had left by now, except for a sour-looking man who stood across the street. He had watched with interest as Ben and Jim had talked, as if to catch a word or two they had exchanged. Jim wasn't the only nosy person in town, Ben surmised. As he closed the door to the patrol car, he glanced back only to see that the man had vanished. Though he had only taken his eyes away for a second or two, there was no sign of him anywhere on the street. Guess he was more exhausted than he thought. This was going to be a tough week or so, no doubt.

He would need a lot of support the next couple of weeks, and what better support than his old high school buddies. There were only a couple of guys he hung out with back then, and they were practically inseparable. There was Jim, Dave Burton, and Jack Reed, known to most as Swede, because of his height, blond hair, and imposing presence. Where you found one, you usually found all. With only a couple of exceptions, they took the same classes and could all be found any Friday and Saturday night hanging out at Tasty Freeze or Gook's, the other popular drive-in out on the highway. Jim would be in his dad's Buick, wearing his signature cowboy hat; Jack on his Harley; and Dave in a plain Chevy Biscayne that they used to kid him about. His grandmother's car, they would joke. A look under the hood told another story, however, as he had installed a heavily modified "big block." That made it what they called a sleeper back then.

Ben usually drove his '66 Chevy Impala SS, a car that he had saved long and hard for. He was able to get it long enough to enjoy it before he left for boot camp and looked forward to returning to the States in a few years. The plan was to pick it up and take it along to his next duty assignment then keep it with him throughout his Army career. Jack, on the other hand, wasn't so much a car guy as he was a motorcycle fanatic. For as long as Ben could remember, Jack talked about riding a Harley one day and building as many as he could. While the rest of them were trying to learn history, math, or civics, Jack was sketching Harleys of all flavors. Choppers, dressers, racers, antiques, it didn't matter. They all had the distinctive V-twin engine between the frame rails.

Reality came back as Jim asked, "What are you going to do first when you get to the house? I suspect you'll get something to eat and maybe sleep awhile?"

Ben hadn't thought that far ahead but replied, "Put on some coffee first, and then sit for a bit. There's so much to do. I'll have to get myself organized. By the way, how is it you were at the bus terminal when I got there? Is that part of your patrol?"

Jim laughed. "Like I said, I'm nosy. I like to see who's getting on and off the bus in town. Never know who you might see. Besides, a lot of us knew you'd be coming in, so I figured I'd like to be there when you did. Don't mind, do you?"

"Of course not. Just didn't think I'd get such an 'official' welcome." It was a welcome surprise to see him, Ben thought. All things considered, a familiar face was important right now.

Soon, they rounded Snow's Turn, just outside town and only about fifteen minutes or so to his home. Ben asked, "How is the sheriffing business? Anything like you thought it would be?" He was hoping a little small talk would help delay his arrival at a familiar yet strangely different place.

Jim nodded. "Yep, I like it just fine, better in most ways than I thought it would be. Serve some papers now and then, catch a couple speeders, and break up a few fights, that sort of thing. There's an ugly side too. Domestic disturbances, some with little kids in the middle of 'em. I don't like those. I really like the investigative stuff, though I don't get involved in a lot of that."

"Like what?" Ben asked.

Jim looked a little solemn as he answered, "Just routine stuff. Robberies, accidents, maybe a homicide. The state police usually get into that, though. All I can do is look over their shoulder after they push me out of 'em. But I enjoy snooping around anyway. I just stay out of their way, and they leave me alone."

"Sounds pretty interesting to me." Ben noticed just a small amount of sadness in his voice. "Anything really good going on?"

"How 'bout I stop by tomorrow, after you've had some rest, then maybe we can talk about some stuff I've been looking into." Jim's serious tone indicated there was something bothering him about a case he was on, but he didn't seem to want to turn the conversation in that direction right now. That was okay, since Ben didn't want to hear about anything that might be of consequence either. He had enough to deal with.

"Do you know anything about what happened to my parents?" Ben asked.

"You just got here. You're tired and probably hungry. I'll stop by tomorrow," Jim answered, clearly uneasy at the question that was posed to him. Ben decided to let it go.

They turned off the main road onto a county road, and Ben watched the long driveway to his childhood home come into view. Filled with an almost overwhelming sense of sadness, he inhaled deeply, tensed in his seat, and braced for what used to be a pleasant view he had seen for many years: home.

Jim turned the patrol car onto the long lane that led to the house. About a mile and a half long, it pointed straight to the large home at the end. As the car slowly traveled the dirt and gravel path, Ben gazed at the familiar sight of cattails and marsh grass that lined the right side. They grew along the shallow ditch that marked the property line on the southeast. Here and there, soft rushes and wood reeds filled in, moving gently in the breeze. A little farther up, the old barn could be seen, long since abandoned, its roof bowed in the center and openings in the side where boards used to be. To the rear of the barn, the implement shed stood, with four open bays facing the marsh that crept in, marked by high grasses and more cattails. It appeared the farmer that leased the four hundred or so acres kept some equipment in there still.

Next came the open area, about four acres, where a house once stood. Grass filled the area now, meeting the road, divided by a dirt driveway leading to a small grove of pear trees—twenty-one, to be exact. Ben knew this part of the property well since he was tasked with mowing the grass and raking up all the pears that fell. With no one to care for the orchard, the pears still grew, unfit to eat. If not cleaned up, the rotting pears would begin to smell and attract bees, Dad had said. So once a year, rake and wheelbarrow at hand, Ben would rake and dump, taking about two days to get everything done.

To the left of the long driveway were fields, usually with corn, sometimes with beans. The farmer who took care of all that would alternate crops, and it looked like this year, it was the corn's turn once again. Ben liked the corn crop, mainly because he enjoyed walking through the fields after the harvest, usually headed to the end of the property to what he referred to as the Point, far beyond the house. He could almost hear the Canadian geese flying overhead as they did each fall, heading south to their winter homes.

Unable to delay any longer, Ben looked straight ahead to a place, up until a few hours ago, he had longed to see. It was supposed to be a happy return, one that he had anticipated after his tour in Europe had ended. A couple of weeks' leave and time to visit old friends, then off to his next unit. By all accounts, his visit home should have been about a year away. His current duty extension had been approved, and he looked forward to an extra year in Germany to travel, enjoy time with the friends he had made, and submit his paperwork to apply for Warrant Officer. Plans had been made carefully and with considerable thought, all to lay the groundwork for what he hoped would be a rewarding Army career. It could all be salvaged with some minor changes in those plans, but right now, other, more pressing business lay ahead.

His boyhood home loomed among the red maples, water oaks, and holly trees that surrounded it. The dirt road that they had traveled so far became blacktop as it approached the front of the house, forming a sort of teardrop shape, returning to connect to the lane. Off to the left, a wider paved area lay before the four-car garage.

"Well, this is new," he said out loud. "Dad always talked about paving the whole road one day. Guess this is as far as he got."

Jim nodded. "Looks pretty good. Be easy to clean the snow off of it this winter." Though they hadn't said much for most of the trip, Jim was getting ready to wrap things up for now. "Well, here you are, buddy. Anything else I can do for you?"

"No, thanks. You've done plenty. Guess I'll hear from you?" There was a tone of hope in Ben's question.

"Sure thing. I'll call you tomorrow, maybe stop by if you're around. Number still the same?"

Ben nodded. "Yeah, far as I know. Got some phone calls to make, but I expect to be here. Thanks again. It was good to see a friend first thing."

"No sweat, buddy. I'll be in touch." Jim handed him a business card. "Wrote my home phone on the back. Call me anytime. Use the official number if you need to. They'll get hold of me on the radio."

"Thanks. I'll hang on to this," Ben said as he grabbed his bag from the back of the car. "See ya later."

"Later, my friend," replied Jim as he put the car in gear and slowly drove away.

Ben watched as the car disappeared down the road in a small cloud of dust. Soon, he realized he hadn't even turned toward the house as the car finally left his view, turning onto the county road. Duffel bag at his feet, he turned to survey his home. It was an imposing house—two and a half stories tall, with four columns rising from the shallow porch to meet the edge of the roof far above. It always reminded him of a Southern plantation-style home, though he had only seen those on TV. Clean white siding was accented by black shutters at each window, even beside the three dormer windows that jutted from the roof. The main front door was windowless, painted red, with a large brass knocker in the center. On each side, narrow windows rose to the height of the door.

On the east side, to the right of the main house, a two-story addition was attached, dressed to match the rest of the home. That was originally the maid's quarters when the house was built, sometime back in the twenties. Now, it contained the laundry room, kitchen, and mudroom, with a narrow stairway leading to a small, apartment-size bedroom, bath, and sitting area.

To the west stood a two-story, four-car garage. The second floor, used for storage, was unfinished. Below, a neatly organized workbench ran the full length of the back wall, with a pegboard tool arrangement and cabinets that held various tools and other gadgets needed for vehicle maintenance. Each bay had a window that overlooked the backyard, which, when opened, allowed a breeze to cool the work areas.

Ben turned from the main door and went instead to the kitchen door to his right. He almost always entered and exited this way when he lived here. Mom would usually get upset if he tracked mud or dirt through the living room. Though his shoes were clean now, Ben felt it seemed a little late to change habits. Without giving it any thought, he reached behind the lamp beside the door and removed a small metal container that held the door key. He unlocked the door and went inside.

The kitchen was eerily quiet, which Ben had expected. The only TV in the house was here, on a shelf over the counter. They didn't watch much TV when he was growing up here as Dad always believed there was too much to do and far more interesting things with which they all could occupy their time. In spite of that, Mom and Dad would watch some news, weather, and an occasional show while they enjoyed a snack or a cup of coffee. They rarely used the formal dining room next to the kitchen, instead choosing the intimacy of the kitchen table. The small kitchen table was flanked on one side with a marble countertop, in which a double porcelain sink was installed. The right side of the counter ended at a stovetop and oven. Above it all were cabinets made of light-colored pine and finished with sturdy chrome pulls. At the rear of the kitchen, a door opened to the patio, and a window looked out into the yard. A window on the front wall gave a clear view of the yard beyond, as well as most of the long driveway.

He set his bag on the floor and pulled out a chair. Sitting slowly, he looked around with sadness at the thought of never being able to share time with his parents again. Ben did his homework here, shared his many car magazines with his dad here, and together, they dreamed of a hot rod they would one day build together. Mom would smile and shake her head as she slid a plate of a freshly baked cake in front of them. "Don't get any grease on the table," she would say.

To keep any tears from falling, he got up and went to the coffeepot. Coffee always seemed to help ease any stresses that came along, so maybe it would work this time too. Ben didn't drink and rarely consumed anything other than coffee, milk, or iced tea. Dad always believed one should always keep their wits about them, and you couldn't do that if you were full of alcohol. That philosophy seemed to work for him, so it was good enough for Ben.

Soon the smell of fresh coffee filled the room, so Ben took a cup from the cabinet overhead, spooned in a little sugar, and filled it with the fresh brew. Normally, he and Dad would sit and talk, but today, Ben decided it would be best to change things up a little bit. He wasn't used to sitting here alone, so he took his cup and left the kitchen through the door of the mudroom and walked toward the pier.

Fishing Creek surrounded three sides of their property, making the land a bit of a peninsula. This side tapered to little more than a ditch behind the old barn he had passed, but the pier extended about fifty feet out into the widest part. The far shore was about three hundred feet away from its end, giving plenty of room for small boats to pass by. Near the end of the pier sat two Adirondack chairs with a small wooden table between them. Ben sat his cup on the table and settled into the one on his left. That was where Dad always sat when he and Mom went out to enjoy a quiet evening together.

Tied to the left side of the pier was Dad's boat. It was a seventeen-foot Dorsett Catalina. The turquoise paint looked fresh, even though the fiberglass was laid in 1961. With a small cabin and a forty-horsepower Mercury outboard engine, it provided all the fun the family needed for a day on the water. "How many trips to Cambridge had we made in that boat?" Ben wondered. Dad usually put it up for the winter at a storage location in town, so he must have only recently put it in the water, in anticipation of another boating season.

On the right side of the pier was the old skiff Ben used to take out for fishing and crabbing. He used to joke about how slow it was, being built from oak that must have weighed a couple of tons. With a four-horsepower Sears outboard and a flat bottom, it was safe for his purposes, though sailboats could pass him by on a calm day. He had a lot of fun in that boat. It remained in the water all year, with no chance of damage from what little ice might form here in the shallows. They would just bail it out once in a while and let it go.

A warm breeze came from the south and gently moved the cattails and soft rush that grew beside the creek. Now and then, he could hear a couple of geese overhead, flying to the rhythm of the waves softly tapping the shore beneath him. It would soon be time to go back inside as he could feel fatigue begin to overtake him. He decided to close his eyes for a moment.

*****

Ben parked his Volkswagen Bug in front of a small house on the outskirts of Herzogenaurach, just a couple of miles from the base. He was a bit anxious about this, his first date with Allie. Dinner, then a walk around Nurnberg, was on this evening's agenda, and he hoped it would go well. Should they go to a Gasthaus or to a nice restaurant? The Gasthaus would be less formal, given the patrons being local people, but the food was always good, the atmosphere brighter, and sometimes, it was a little loud. There were plenty of really nice restaurants in the city, though he had never been to one. He had passed by several during his many trips to see the sights but was reluctant to dine alone in such places, but that might seem a little pretentious and maybe too intimate for a first date. *Guess I'll just wing it*, he thought.

Before he could get out of the car, he saw the door of the house open. Standing on the sidewalk, he watched as Allie emerged. He had never seen her in civilian clothes before and was a little stunned as she approached him, wearing a bright smile. While most young women chose to wear "the style of the day," such as bell-bottom pants, some leather something adorned with fringe, and a tie-dyed shirt (at least that was the way Ben saw them), Allie wore knee-high brown leather boots, jeans, and a loose-fitting white sweater. Tiny diamond earrings glimmered in the sunlight, partially hidden beneath her shiny brown hair. He had never seen her hair down before, as Army requirements dictated that it must be pulled up in such a way to fit under the uniform headgear. Ben thought she couldn't have been more beautiful the first time he saw her, but somehow she succeeded in topping that first meeting. *They sure grow 'em different in New Mexico*, Ben thought.

"Hi there, Sergeant! Been looking forward to tonight," she said. Her brown eyes twinkled as her smile turned into a chuckle.

"Well hello, Specialist Morgan. Me, too," Ben answered. In his mind, he was wondering if maybe he could really pull this off and make it an enjoyable evening. He hadn't dated since high school, and as a kid, he figured he had an excuse if things went wrong. But this was the real deal with a real woman and nobody to call for help if things got a little wacky. Before any more doubt could overtake him, he opened the passenger-side door for her, and then, after she was seated, closed it, took his place behind the wheel, and pulled away from the curb.

A horn blew from behind them, startling him for a moment. It was only after it blew again that he realized he was partially awake, and someone had pulled into the driveway.

CHAPTER 2

Still groggy from his unexpected nap, Ben stood and looked toward the driveway. A dark-blue Lincoln stood before the house, and someone was emerging from the front door. He immediately recognized that someone as Mr. Sterling, the family attorney. He stood erect, revealing his imposing stature. With Mr. Sterling being over six feet tall, his height was accentuated by his thin frame. Just as Ben remembered him, he wore a dark-blue three-piece suit with a matching tie and now carried a brown leather briefcase. Ben always thought the way he dressed up was just a show, perhaps adding an air of importance to the way he presented himself. And that suit wasn't one that could be found at the local department store, maybe not even in the best clothing store nearby. Sometimes, in the past, he would be quick to remind you that his suits came from only the best shops in New York.

Ben never really liked him much, either. Though Mr. Sterling must be a highly qualified attorney, he had a creepiness about him that just didn't sit well. More than once, when Mr. Sterling was at the house, conducting whatever business he and Dad shared, Ben would see him watching Mom in a way that was unfitting for a friend or business associate. He would follow her every move and seem unattached from the task at hand, then look away quickly if she were to glance his way. Kind of gave Ben the chills.

And he wasn't a handsome man either. Tall, thin, almost gaunt, he looked better suited as a mortician or butler in a haunted house. His eyes always darted about, looking, no doubt, for a body that he had perhaps misplaced. You couldn't look at him, and you dared not look away. "Hope this doesn't last long," Ben wished to himself.

"Good afternoon, Master Ben," he said, as he stretched out his hand. "You look well. Was your trip home without difficulty?"

"Hello, Mr. Sterling. Yes, yes, it was okay, I guess. I don't like to fly, you know. But I guess sometimes you just have to. I was going to call you today." As much as he hated it, Ben knew that sooner or later they would have to meet.

"I won't keep you. I'm sure you have much to do. I just wanted to welcome you home and drop off some papers for your perusal. I also have taken the liberty of making a few arrangements to help ease your burden. Please accept my condolences for your loss. Your parents were such fine people, and I feel fortunate to have called them friends. I suspect you may have some questions for me as well?" he asked with a raised eyebrow.

Ben motioned toward the house and answered, "Sure. Come on in, and we can sit at the kitchen table."

Ben led the way, and soon, at the table, Mr. Sterling removed several folders from his briefcase. Some seemed to hold only a few papers, others bulging with documents that must have been of some importance.

"I have to know, Mr. Sterling, what happened. Nobody has told me anything. How it happened, where, why. Nothing." It was almost a demand, but Ben needed to know. And he didn't care if Mr. Sterling was uncomfortable answering or not.

Mr. Sterling sat back in his chair with his hands clasped. "Well, Master Ben, there was an accident on the Choptank Bridge. They were on their way back from Washington and went off the bridge. No one is sure exactly what happened, but they went into the river. Apparently, the bridge span was open, and Arthur didn't see it. You know, how the center span pivots to let ships go through? Anyway, they went off the end, must have hit the center concrete support, and went down. I suspect it happened pretty fast. They had been reported missing by one of your father's friends, and it was only because a fisherman saw what appeared to be an automobile down there that a search was conducted and they were found. Guess it had happened a couple days before."

Ben tried hard to get out of his mind the picture that had just been painted by the attorney. "Wait a minute. What about the gates, the warning lights? The gates should have been down, the lights flashing. Dad should have seen that. Were they working? Does anybody know?"

Mr. Sterling shook his head. "That was all investigated. Everything was working fine. And your father had not been drinking. He never drank when he knew he had to drive anywhere. And he was on some kind of official business in DC that evening. From what I understand, a business/pleasure kind of trip. That's why Mila, Ms. Mila, was along." He always referred to Ben's mom as Ms. Mila and changed his reference to her quickly. *Too quickly*, Ben thought.

This was the first time anyone had given him anything like a detail about how his parents died. Maybe that's why Jim didn't want to talk about it earlier.

The attorney continued, "Look, we can talk about those things another time. Perhaps I can go over some formalities with you.

I'll leave some papers with you to look over and contact you tomorrow."

"Yeah, okay." As far as he was concerned, the meeting was over. Ben didn't feel like talking or listening to anything. Nothing was that important right now. But the sooner this guy left, the better. Ben just wanted to be alone and certainly not be entertained by the mortician.

With Ben only half-listening, Mr. Sterling explained the will, estate issues, obituaries, caskets, funerals, relatives, and other details Ben didn't even pay attention to.

As a thought came to him, Ben blurted out, "What about Duke? Is he still around? Where is he?"

"Relax," the attorney assured him. "He's being cared for. I saw to that. I'll arrange for him to be brought to you when you're ready."

"Thanks." Ben was relieved. Duke was a purebred German shepherd, beautifully marked and intelligent. It would be good to see him again. Though he must have grown to his full adult size, he would nevertheless be a familiar member of the family that Ben needed right now. Though Duke was only about a year old when Ben left for boot camp, they were nearly inseparable. Whether it was fishing, crabbing, a boat ride, or just running through the fields, Duke was at his side. Though he had a good disposition, he was very protective of not only Ben but Mom and Dad also. It was clear he didn't care for Dad's attorney either, as he would always sit nearby, eyes glued to him, and sometimes, let out a soft growl. Sometimes, even his hair would stand on end. Ben thought it was funny, but Dad would give the dog a stern look and shake his finger at him. Duke usually paid him no mind and continued his vigil. It wasn't lost on Mr. Sterling. As his eyes darted around the room, he would remain fixed for just a second longer on the dog, who was studying him.

"I shall leave you now. Look those things over and call me. My card is stapled to the top folder. I'm available at any time for you. Is there anything else I can do for you?" Mr. Sterling asked as he stood and closed his briefcase.

"No, I'll give you a call if I have any questions. I'm going into town tomorrow and get started on some of the arrangements. There's some people I'll need to contact. Do you know anything about Mom's sister? Has she been notified?" Ben asked.

The attorney shook his head. "No, but her number is in the top folder. I can call her, if you'd like."

"I'll do it. Should come from family, I think." Ben dreaded making the phone call, but it had to be done. Dad had no living relatives, but Mom had a sister in Belgium. He wasn't sure if she would come all the way to the States, but he had to give her the opportunity.

"So be it. I'll hear from you?" Mr. Sterling asked as he went toward the door.

"Yeah, sure." Ben felt relieved the mortician man was leaving.

The attorney let himself out as Ben looked at the pile of papers on the table. *These can wait a bit*, he thought. *I'll get myself organized this evening and hit the ground running tomorrow.* There was enough to digest for one day already, and a good night's rest would give him a clearer head, which will be needed the next several days.

Though it was still light outside and too early for bed under normal circumstances, Ben decided that he'd turn in. He locked the kitchen door, turned out the light, and slowly walked upstairs to the tiny bedroom. A small clock radio sat on a bedside table, and he turned it on and found a station playing mild rock music. With the volume barely audible, he threw himself onto the bed and closed his eyes to Marvin Gaye singing "What's Going On." *What's going on, indeed,* he thought to himself as he almost immediately fell into a deep sleep.

*****

Allie stood before him, tears shimmering on her cheeks as she emerged from the shadows. She reached one hand toward him and took a cautious step forward, but instead of going closer, she moved a step farther away. Behind him, Ben heard quiet sobbing and turned to see his mother, head bowed, holding a silk handkerchief to her face. Beside her stood his father, one arm around his bride, his head buried in her hair, tears visible on his cheek.

He turned to Allie, called her name, but no sound came out. He turned again, toward his parents, called to them, but once again, no voice could be heard emanating from his mouth. He moved toward them, and they drifted away, as if enveloped in a fog. Then, turning, he reached out to Allie, but she, too, disappeared as if she were merely a wisp of smoke.

Suddenly he found himself alone, no one before him, no one behind. Then, blackness.

*****

Ben woke to see daylight creeping into his small room. The clock said 7:00 a.m., and just for a second, he panicked. The physical-training formation was called at six, and he was still in bed. It sure wouldn't go well to come dragging out after the commander took charge of the company. By the time his feet hit the floor, he realized where he was and felt embarrassed. Foolishly he looked around to make sure no one saw his shock.

Well, he was wide-awake now. Might as well get up and get this day started.

After cleaning up, brushing his teeth, and making the bed, he slipped on some jeans and a T-shirt and went down to the kitchen and put on some coffee. He checked the local news channel for a weather report and then made some toast. Sooner or later, he'd have to eat something substantial, but he could run into town later to get something.

As he ate his toast and sipped some coffee, he looked over the papers that Mr. Sterling had left with him. The first folder contained his parents' will, and he could look at that later. The next held obituaries for each of them that the attorney had taken the liberty to complete. He'd look at those later too. The next folder contained what appeared to be legal papers relating to property, bank accounts, and phone numbers of people Ben didn't know. That could wait also. The last folder contained a single document that contained contact information for Ben, as well as his aunt in Belgium. He pushed the other folders aside and laid the last folder in front of him. He knew he'd have to call his aunt soon and sure didn't look forward to it. He checked the time and determined he had a few hours before the time difference made it impractical. Best wait until the end of her day to be sure to catch her at home.

Ben took his coffee cup and walked to the door leading to the dining room. As he entered the room, he felt an emptiness he had never felt before. Quiet, with the TV in the kitchen barely audible, he walked slowly, admiring the furniture, paintings on each wall, and the flowers his mother had so lovingly cared for.

He then entered the living room. Neatly arranged Victorian-style furniture was arrayed in such a way that, no matter where you sat, you would be facing someone else. Dad wanted it that way for entertaining. In one corner stood his mother's favorite item: an antique record player that Dad had restored for her. The electronics had been updated inside, yet the exterior kept its original appearance. On the turntable rested a record Dad had given her for their first anniversary. Written in the late 1800s, the opera *La Bohème* was a favorite of hers. Ben almost knew it by heart as she played it all the time and refused to remove it from the record player. Ben turned and walked toward the garage entry door on the other side of a grand staircase.

He opened the door and saw just what he expected to see. The first bay contained his mother's station wagon, clean and ready for any trip she might want to take. In the second bay was his dad's pickup. It was also clean and shiny, looking like it just rolled off the assembly line. The third bay was empty. Dad kept his "business" sedan there. Though he had retired from the Army, he still attended meetings now and then and used that car for such things. That must be what he was driving when they had the accident. In the last bay, under a custom cover, was Ben's Impala.

He walked to the rear of the garage and set his cup on the workbench. Passing tools, drawers, and his and dad's tool chests, he went to the car. Pulling the cover off, he welcomed the sight of it. Clean as the others, the car would be ready to drive just as it sat. Ben glanced at the rear wall and was reassured by the four clipboards that hung in the same order as that of the vehicles they represented. Even the empty bay had its own clipboard. It contained service information for the boat motors, lawn tractor, and anything else that had an engine and was kept in the small shed out back.

As Ben removed the Impala clipboard from its hanger, he reviewed the information the papers contained. Dad had inspected the car just last month, changed the oil, and given it a short test drive. His initials attested to the car's condition and when the next inspection was due. That was just the way he was. Ben had to smile. Dad always said, "When you work hard to attain the things you want or need, those things deserve attention and care."

"You'll get some fresh air later," Ben whispered, as if the car could hear him.

A knock on the far kitchen door brought Ben back from his thoughts. It was still early, so he couldn't imagine who might be here already.

Glancing through the front window on his way to the kitchen, he saw a bright-red Corvette in the driveway. "That could be anybody," he figured. He knew he would soon find out.

No sooner than Ben opened the door had a giant of a dog bounded through, practically knocking him over. The dog ran past the kitchen and disappeared through the door to the dining room. Still watching, Ben heard a female voice behind him.

"Sorry, I didn't think he'd do that," said the young blond woman who stood there. "Forgive me?" she asked.

"Sure," Ben replied. "I know you, don't I?"

"Yes, we went to high school together," she stated.

"Sarah. Sarah Dempsey. Been a while." Ben invited her in, just as the dog rounded the corner and slid into the kitchen. "Duke! Is this Duke?"

"Yep, that's him. I've been watching him the past week or so," she said as Duke stopped in front of her. "He's a bit spoiled, you know. Not all my doing, really."

Sarah Dempsey. Ben remembered her from school—an attractive girl who grew into a striking young woman. Blond hair, blue eyes, a slight tan. In tight white jeans and a tighter white T-shirt, she looked like a magazine ad for tanning lotion. Ben remembered that she always had a tan, even during the cold months. He suspected some might be from the sun, but the rest from an application of some sort, a drugstore tan, maybe. She never gave Ben and his friends the time of day back then, as she preferred athletes or sons of wealthy parents. Either would do until she got tired of them and moved on to the next. Ben's Dad used to say, "Everybody thinks that what they're looking at is the best thing they've ever seen until they see something better."

Yep, that was Sarah. She could have been beautiful if she had not tried so hard to be pretty. Ben was always glad he never made her short list.

"I sure appreciate that you took care of him. He's kind of a 'people dog,' you know. He likes to have a companion human," Ben said sincerely.

"No problem. Mr. Sterling is my dad's attorney, as well, and he asked us to look after him until you got here," she explained.

"I hope he was no trouble, big as he is. Last time I saw him, he was only about half this size," Ben said.

By now, Duke seemed to recognize Ben and whimpered as he put his giant feet on Ben's shoulders. Eye to eye now, Ben could see that everything would be okay with him. He was home, and they could get to know each other again.

"No trouble at all. Do you need anything?" she asked. "You know I'm just across the creek."

"No, thanks," Ben replied. "I think we'll be okay."

"Okay," she said with a smile. Handing him a small piece of paper, she said coyly, "Call me anytime. I can be here in five minutes."

"Sure. Thanks," Ben said.

With one of those little finger waves, she walked back to her car, glancing back with a smile as she went. Ben looked at Duke. "Well, buddy, are you glad to be home?" Duke just looked back at him and barked. It seemed he was.

*****

After a quick shower, Ben and Duke were on their way to town. It felt good to be behind the wheel of his car, his dog in the front seat, head out the partially open window, as dogs like to do. For just a few moments, Ben was able to put reality aside and enjoy the warm spring morning. There was still much to do, most of it unpleasant, but at least for the time being, everything else was out of his mind.

Little traffic was on the road, and the black sedan that followed from a distance was not even noticed by the pair as they motored along. The two men inside didn't speak. They simply looked ahead at the Impala and kept far enough behind so as not to be conspicuous but close enough to remain in sight.

As Ben and Duke pulled into the parking lot of the all-night diner on the highway, the sedan parked across the road beside a gas station. From here, they could watch the car they had been carefully tailing without being noticed.

Ben went inside the diner, leaving Duke in the car, watching him anxiously. He soon emerged with a small bag containing breakfast for both himself and his companion. As they each enjoyed a scrapple and egg sandwich, Ben with orange juice and Duke with a cup of water, they frequently exchanged glances. Duke was clearly happy at the moment, either because Ben was with him once again or just because he liked the typical Eastern Shore breakfast. It really didn't matter right now. They both needed breakfast.

After a small but welcome meal, Ben left the diner and drove into town. Familiar sights greeted him as they traveled down the main street, south toward the road home. There were a few people about, none he recognized, and he guessed that soon the streets would be busy with people going about their daily business.

The visit to the funeral home went quickly, as Mr. Sterling had already set things in motion before Ben's arrival. The matching caskets were the best available, in dark walnut trimmed with ornate brass. It was one of the most difficult things he had ever done, so he was grateful that he needed to spend only minimal time there. The funeral was set for noon on Saturday, and there was plenty of room for the anticipated visitors. Besides the many friends of the family, there were numerous military officers and staff his dad had worked with who were expected to be there. After signing a few papers and thanking the funeral director, Ben returned to the car and headed home.

His mind racing, Ben soon turned onto the county road leading to his lane, a black sedan pulling off some distance behind. Arriving at the house, he left the car in the driveway, watching Duke race around the yard. To the left (west side of the house), a line of closely planted decorative pine trees formed a windbreak that extended far into the backyard before turning right to head toward the creek. The line of trees also served to define the well-kept yard as well as separate it from the fields that lay beyond. Ben briefly considered taking a walk through the field out to what he called the Point, as he had done so many times in his boyhood. There would be time for that later, Ben thought, so he called for Duke, and they went into the house.

He heated up a cup of coffee, left over from earlier this morning, and sat at the kitchen table, under Duke's watchful eye. As the dog settled down, lying at his feet, Ben chose a folder from the stack that awaited his attention. This one contained his parents' will. Glancing through the pages of legalese, he saw references to property and monetary assets, with his name mentioned now and then. He figured he might need Mr. Sterling's interpretation for all this. He dug out the folder containing property and account information and, placing it with the will, pushed it aside.

He looked at the folder of phone numbers and then at the clock. He figured noon would be the best time to call his aunt. That only gave him a couple of hours to prepare himself for delivering the news to his mom's sister. In spite of the miles between them, they were very close. Aunt Louise and her daughter had visited a few times in the past, visits that Ben enjoyed. Her stories and laughter filled the house, and Mom beamed every minute Louise was here. This call wasn't going to be easy.

As Ben pondered what he was going to say to her and how to say it, a tan Chevy sedan pulled into the driveway. Through the window, he could see that it was another high school friend, Dave Burton. He couldn't make out the passenger but could see that it was a tall male. As they exited the car, he saw that the passenger was his other friend, Jack Reed. Smiling, Ben opened the kitchen door and stepped outside, Duke close behind.

The dog reached them before Ben could even say a word. Duke sniffed one then the other, barked a couple of times, and ran back, as if to indicate they were okay with him.

"Hey, guys! Come on in. It's good to see you." Ben was genuinely excited to see them both. It had been a long time.

Dave spoke first. "Figured you might need a little help around here while you're home. So here we are."

"Yeah," Jack added, "anything you need, when you need it. That's us."

"Well, thank you. You guys want some coffee or something else?" Ben remembered that neither of the guys drank anything heavier than a soda, at least back when they hung out.

"I'll take some coffee. How 'bout you, Jackson?" Dave always seemed to prefer full names when addressing someone. That hadn't changed.

"I'm good. Maybe something after a while." Jack settled into a chair, followed by Dave in another. Duke sat by the door so he could keep an eye on all of them.

Over the next several minutes, they caught up on things that had happened in the last four years since they had seen one another last. Jack had opened a motorcycle shop where he built custom bikes. He also formed a small motorcycle club made up of like-minded riders.

Dave, the resident genius, had gone to college but dropped out because, as he put it, he "forgot more about physics and quantum theory than they ever knew." So he went home and became a consultant in just about any subject or area anyone needed.

Ben could have predicted Jack's career choices as he had lived and breathed motorcycles for as long as he could remember. Dave, on the other hand, was tough to figure out. One minute he was frantically scratching out calculations that could be understood by no one but him; the next minute, he was under the hood of his car, trying to squeeze more horsepower out of it. Go figure.

Jack switched to his serious mode. "How are you doin', bud? We were really sorry to hear about your folks. We had a lot of fun here back then, and your folks really took good care of us."

"I'm doing okay, I guess. All things considered." *Not entirely true*, Ben thought. But having his friends here sure helped.

Ben looked at the clock. He'd have to call his aunt soon, no avoiding it much longer.

"Excuse me for a couple minutes, guys. I have to make a phone call. And don't leave yet, help yourself to the coffee and fridge." He figured he'd need a little support after this call.

Ben returned to the kitchen half an hour later to see that Jim had joined the group. As they all grew silent and looked at Ben, they could see he was not as jocular as before. "Hey, Jim" was all he said.

They sat in silence for a while until Ben finally spoke up.

"Had to call my aunt and give her the news. She took it pretty hard. Guess she'll be flying in tomorrow, if she can get a flight."

"Give me her flight details when you get 'em, and I'll pick her up at the airport. You've got plenty to do, and she knows me from her visits here in the past," Jim stated. "Discussion over. Jack, come with me." Ben had to smile. The last time Aunt Louise came to visit, she brought her daughter, Olivia, with her. With Olivia at just a year younger than Jim, they hit it off almost immediately. He was attracted to her, and she to him. They spent as much time together as her mother would allow them and insisted they not be alone with each other. So with Ben riding along, they went for short drives around the lower county and even went on a boat ride or two. It was clear they enjoyed each other's company, and it didn't hurt that Aunt Louise took a liking to Jim as well. Besides, Mom knew his parents well and vouched for him as a responsible young man with a promising future in law enforcement.

"I'll be ready, bud." Jack stood up to leave. "Come on, Dave. Let's go." Looking at Ben, he added, "Call me if you need to. I'll likely see you tomorrow or the day after."

"Sure, man. Take care. You, too, Dave. Thanks for coming by." Ben was truly grateful.

After they left, Jim said to Ben, "Let's take a walk, bud. Want to run some stuff by you."

"You sound serious," Ben replied.

"Yep." Seemed he was serious.

With Duke running ahead, Jim and Ben walked around the hedgerow toward the Point. The air was warm, and the smell of the marsh grasses was faint as they walked quietly along.

"Did anybody tell you about the accident your folks had?" Jim asked hesitantly.

Ben replied, "Yeah, Mr. Sterling told me about it. Not a lot of detail, but enough to know what happened."

"Didn't it sound a little odd, what happened, I mean?" It was clear Jim didn't accept the circumstances surrounding the wreck.

"Well, yeah. I had a couple questions, but he implied that the investigation confirmed what happened pretty much." Ben was getting a little confused by Jim's questions. "Why? What do you know about it?"

"Well, some stuff just don't add up." Jim continued by explaining that the warning lights and gates on the bridge had been checked out and were working normally. The weather had been clear; there was no alcohol or drugs found in his dad's blood work, and the autopsy found no signs of medical problems that would have caused him to lose control of the car.

Furthermore, the bridge operator stated that he had not been on call that night and had, in fact, not opened the bridge for anyone in over a week leading up to the time they determined the crash had occurred. The police had closed the investigation and determined it was simply an unfortunate accident.

"Kind of weird, don't you think, Ben, old buddy?"

Ben was speechless at that point.

Jim continued with some other unusual things that had happened around the county lately. Four teenagers had gone missing, as well as two experienced watermen. The teenagers had been last seen in town but had told everyone they were going to the same place: DeCoursey Bridge, in the southern part of the county. Kids liked to take their girlfriends to the bridge where, legend had it, you could see a ghost if you shut your car engine off while sitting on the bridge around midnight. One couple had gone missing several weeks ago; the other, late last week. The watermen had also disappeared over the course of a couple of weeks with no trace. It appeared that one minute they were motoring along out in the bay and then simply vanished. There were no signs of them anywhere: no fuel spill, debris, no bits of wreckage.

"What are you saying, Jim? You think this might all be related in some way?"

"Maybe." Jim didn't seem fully convinced himself, but Ben could see the wheels turning in his head.

They walked in silence to the point, looked over the creek, then turned toward home.

Ben had confidence in Jim's investigative abilities, but this seemed a little far-fetched. It was a bit intriguing, but he'd have to think about this for a bit.

After returning to the house, Jim told him they'd talk again later and left. Ben and Duke went inside, and after a quick snack, they retired to the living room and sat in the quiet, watching the night creep in. Sleep came easy this night, and Ben enjoyed a dreamless rest as the events of the last few days finally caught up to him.

CHAPTER 3

There was a spot on a lonely road in the southern part of the county from which you could look out over the Chesapeake Bay. The road wound along the marshes, turning sharply in many places, as if searching for solid ground to cling to. A few miles offshore, in the shallows near the shipping lanes, sat the rusted hulk of what was once a large cargo ship. Scuttled or just sunk during a storm, its bow pointed upward from the surf, as if trying to escape its permanent resting place. The stern lay only a few feet below the surface, stuck forever in the grasp of the shifting sand and sediment it called home.

On this night, only a ghostly silhouette could be seen in the moonlight. An unlikely destination, no matter the time of day, it presented itself as an unwelcome specter on this calm, chilly night.

The damp, salty air penetrated Sarah's jacket and chilled her as if winter had waited just for her on this night. She had taken this ride on several other occasions but never got used to it. It seemed like so much useless drama, having to meet the boss this way, but the pay was good, and she liked the lifestyle this aspect of her job offered. A paralegal by day, a mysterious modern-day spy by night. It did provide some excitement in an otherwise-dull world, and you never knew who you might meet. A little drama was a small price to pay.

The small boat slowed as it approached the partially sunken stern, and the motor went silent as it drifted to the rusted giant hull. With a grating noise, a small door opened to reveal a dimly lit hallway, with a red glow lighting the entrance. As always, she stepped out from the bow onto the wide sill as the boat that delivered her backed quietly away.

As Sarah stepped into the hall, the rusty door closed behind her. The dim red glow from the entry lights gave way to soft yellow lamps that introduced a surreal interior. Gleaming white floors and walls were oriented level, not tilted as one might expect from the outside view. Every twenty feet or so, a few steps rose to the next level, each level containing a door on each side behind which some secret hid. At the fifth level, the hallway turned to the left, and an unmarked door faced her. To the right of the door, a small push button was mounted, and she pushed it three short times. She heard the lock release, gently pushed on the door, and stepped inside.

It was a deceptively large room with dark mahogany walls, indirect lighting, and a thick maroon pile carpet. Beautiful paintings with ornate frames lined the walls, punctuated with brass sea-related decorations. A dark-brown leather couch rested against the right wall, with two matching chairs on the left side. Straight ahead, dominating the room, an intricately carved large desk stood to greet any who visited here. An inkwell, a small desk lamp, and a black telephone were all that sat on the desk, making it seem even larger than it was.

Behind the desk, as always, sat the Boss, his back turned to her as he looked out a tiny porthole into the darkness beyond. The high-back leather chair blocked all but the very top of his head. Now and then, a wisp of cigar smoke curled up into the dimness. To Sarah, it looked like his head might be on fire, but she dared not giggle or comment on it.

After a moment of silence, the Boss spoke.

"How are you tonight, my dear?"

Here we go, she thought. Same games.

"Fine, Boss. It's a privilege to be here, sir." Already, she could feel her stomach beginning to turn as the games began.

"Wonderful. Do you enjoy our intimate time together?" Another puff of smoke escaped from his burning head.

"Oh, yes, Boss. It makes me feel tingly all over." She felt tingly, alright, but not in a good way.

"We'll have to get together some day, other than for business, you know? You'd like that, wouldn't you?"

She could hear the anticipation in his voice. "Yes, Boss. That would be so wonderful."

"There will be time for that later," he said, his tone growing a little more serious. "I have a mission for you, my dear girl. Listen carefully. This must be done with the utmost care and attention. Do you understand?"

"Yes, sir," she replied.

"I want you to keep an eye on our little soldier boy. Get close to him, do whatever it takes. I want to know where he goes, who he sees, what he knows. You'll hear from me periodically, and I expect updates each time. Your mission could change at a moment's notice, so be prepared and available. Everything he says, does, and knows is important, so I'll rely on that pretty little brain of yours to give me the details I'll need. You understand? Don't make me have to do something we'll both regret later." He was serious, and she knew it. Somehow, she suspected there were others who had regrets when it came to dealing with this man.

"I understand, sir." No doubt she did.

"Go away now, and leave me to my work. I'll be in touch." Another puff of smoke from his head, and she knew the conversation was over.

Without answering, she turned and left the room. This was her favorite part of their meetings—the moment she left this evil place. On the boat ride back to shore, she felt a sense of foreboding she had never felt before. She had sold her soul to the devil a while ago and knew she had gone too far to quit now. He wouldn't allow it. Besides, living the good life was a small price to pay for doing his bidding. Others weren't so fortunate, and she didn't want to think of how many she had helped meet their misfortunes at her hand. But sometimes, you had to do what you had to do to get ahead in this world. And this mission would be easy. And kind of fun, as well. She couldn't wait to get started.

*****

The morning sun lit the living room, and both Ben and Duke stirred from their sound sleep. Ben, in his dad's favorite recliner, and Duke, beside him on the floor, looked at each other to say a silent "good morning." Duke rose, stretched, and yawned, as did his master. Ben went to the front door and opened it to let his dog run for a bit, then Ben went to the kitchen and put on a pot of coffee.

Louise and Olivia would be flying in this afternoon and would surely be tired and hungry. He had relayed their flight information to Jim last night and was relieved to know they would be picked up at the airport and taken to the house by someone they knew and trusted. A quick check of the fridge revealed that a trip to the grocery store was going to be a priority this morning. Though Ben wasn't much of a cook, he knew that Aunt Louise could help get something together.

He let Duke back into the house through the kitchen door and fed him. He then made a short list for his shopping trip, saw to it that the rest of the house was secure, and closed off the kitchen area for Duke. The dog would sit this trip out, as Ben expected to be in town a little longer today. Locking the door behind him, he got into the Impala, started it, and headed down the long driveway. He looked forward to completing his errands and seeing his aunt later.

Things didn't appear to be busy in town yet, so Ben expected to be able to get his errands done and get home pretty quickly. He went into the local market and picked up what he thought would make a few meals for a couple of days, paid the cashier, and left the store. As he placed his purchases in the back seat of the car, he heard his name called. It was Sarah.

"Well, good morning. Up early this morning, aren't you?" Ben asked. He didn't expect to run into anyone, let alone her, this morning.

"Hello," she replied. "Had to pick some stuff up before work, and this is the only place open. How about you? Kind of early for shopping, isn't it?"

"My aunt is coming in today, so I figured I'd better get some food in the house. Gotta eat, ya know." Ben sat behind the wheel of his car, hoping she wouldn't want to keep talking.

"Say hi for me. She staying long?"

"Don't know. That's up to her. Just have to wait and see." She sure was a nosy one, he thought.

"Well, I just might stop by in a day or so. See you then," she said with a wave.

As he started the car, she turned, smiled, waved again, and then went into the store. He quickly backed away and left the parking lot. He had no intention of getting involved with her. She was bossy, nosy, and liked to take charge of everything. She couldn't be trusted either, from what he remembered from high school. Anyway, he had too much to do in the days ahead and a life to get back to, even if that life was completely altered from what it was less than a week ago.

Soon he was halfway home and planning the day in his mind. A half mile or so behind him, the black sedan kept pace and remained unnoticed.

Ben put the few groceries away and went out into the yard with Duke. Sitting on a bench just outside the door, he watched as the dog ran around the yard, chasing after birds and a squirrel that had come down from a tree. Were it not for the circumstances that brought him home, this would have been a great day to relax and enjoy Duke's company. But any joy he might have let seep into his soul was overshadowed by the reason for his being here. Maybe one day, he thought, but not today.

A small dust cloud at the far end of the road told Ben someone was coming. Soon he could see the red and blue lights on the roof of the car and knew it must be Jim. *Don't tell me he picked up Aunt Louise in his patrol car.* He had to smile at the thought.

Sure enough, Jim pulled the patrol car into the circular driveway, and he could see that his aunt was sitting up front, with Olivia in the back seat, next to Jack. Aunt Louise got out first as soon as the car stopped, and Ben met her before she could take a step. He gave her a big hug, and she returned with a hug of her own. As she began to speak, tears rolled down her cheek.

"Oh, Ben. I'm so sorry. I just can't believe it." She sobbed.

"Me either, Aunt Louise. But we'll get through all this." Ben tried to sound confident, but knew he was failing considerably. "Come on in, and let's get you guys settled."

He turned and gave a hug to Olivia, who had been standing behind him.

"Hello, girl. It's been a long time." He was trying to keep things as light as possible, but that wasn't working either.

"Go on in," Ben said. "I'll get your bags."

Jim and Jack already had their bags and were heading toward the house.

Jack turned to Ben. "Where do you want us to put these?"

"Just set them in the living room, and I'll put them away in a little bit. Just want to get the ladies squared away first. Thanks." Ben would get them settled into their rooms soon, and they could rest up some before getting some supper.

After Jack and Jim had left and the ladies had freshened up a bit, they gathered in the kitchen to talk a bit. Jim had not wanted to leave, and it seemed that Olivia had wanted him to stay awhile, but they both knew they would have some time to catch up tomorrow.

They didn't talk in much detail about the accident or even the upcoming funeral. Instead, they reminisced about the old days, how Ben's mom had met his dad, and the fun they had during those early years together. Louise had been married to a Belgian serviceman who worked with Arthur when he was stationed overseas. Her husband had been killed several years ago during a deployment that was kept secret until his death. Only a few details had been revealed for security reasons. Like Arthur, he worked in high-security areas within the Defense Department and spoke little of his duties. And like Mila, she endured weeks and, sometimes, months without her husband when he would "vanish," as she called it, only to reappear as if nothing ever happened.

He and Arthur had been instrumental in the creation and organization of the Supreme Headquarters Allied Powers Europe, or SHAPE, as it was known around the world. They worked behind the scenes with NATO and other entities to provide information on security issues for the West. Even Ben knew little about what his father did before he retired, only that, on occasion, he would travel to Washington as a civilian, sometimes with Mom, to attend some meeting or dinner event. It seemed that Generals couldn't really retire, especially if they were involved in national security.

Ben fixed a small meal for all of them, and they ate as they talked. Neither of them had much appetite, so sandwiches and sodas were all that were on the menu. Afterward, Ben carried their bags upstairs to the two guest rooms and left Louise and Olivia for the night. Though it was still early, with the sun barely touching the western horizon, they were all weary and ready for a good night's rest.

After letting Duke out once more, he and the dog retired to their room above the kitchen. Climbing into bed, Ben was soon sound asleep, his companion resting on the floor beside him. It would soon prove to be a night without the rest they both needed.

Ben awoke to the sound of Duke whining softly. He looked at the clock and discovered it was only two thirty, far too early for the dog to have to go out. As he looked for Duke in the dim light of the outside security lamp in the front yard, he saw him with his feet on the windowsill, looking over the backyard. His soft whine turned into a soft growl, and his head darted back and forth, as if trying to keep track of something out there.

Ben got up from his bed and crept over to the window.

"Easy, boy. What do you see out there?" he whispered.

Once again, Duke growled softly and looked out across the yard. Though it was quite dark out there as the house blocked any glow from the security light out front, ambient starlight allowed him to make out shadows. One of those shadows began moving toward the river, hugging the tree line at the far end of the yard. Ben could make out the silhouette of a large man standing at the edge of the yard. As the shadow moved again, Ben noticed that he seemed to drag one foot, appearing to have been injured at some point in his life.

Duke growled again, this time a little louder. Afraid the dog might bark, Ben stroked his head and whispered to him again, this time to try to quiet him.

"Stay here, boy," Ben said softly. He quickly got up and opened the door to the stairwell, closing it behind him as he descended the steps to the kitchen below.

Once there, hugging the wall, he opened the pantry door beneath the stairs and reached for what he hoped he would find there.

"Good ol' Dad. Thanks," he said under his breath as he felt the barrel of the shotgun he remembered his father kept there. Checking to see that it was loaded, he was relieved to find that it was ready should he need it.

As Duke growled upstairs, Ben crept to the back window and slowly peeped outside. A second figure rose from close to the side of the house, not three feet away. Moving his head quickly from the window and hugging the wall, Ben hoped he hadn't been seen.

A step and a squeaky, dragging sound revealed this figure was moving away, toward the first shadow he and his dog had seen. There was no time to try to figure out the strange sound he was hearing as the shadows moved toward the river. Ben wanted to know what they were doing and would try to find out as soon as he felt it was safe to do so. He had no inclination to get into a shootout in the middle of the night, especially with two ladies upstairs in the main part of the house.

He moved silently to the end of the hall toward the door leading to the side yard, past the laundry room. He got to the door just in time to see the two shadows climb into a boat with yet a third shadowy figure. They pushed off and moved away from the dock. Though Ben couldn't hear the sound of a motor, the small boat moved smoothly and without sound, northward, around the point, and out of sight.

After opening the stairwell door to allow Duke to join him, Ben carefully went outside to the rear of the house. Holding a flashlight he took from the kitchen counter in one hand and the shotgun in the other, he scanned the ground and windowsills to look for anything unusual. As he did, something at ground level next to the house reflected the beam of the light. Moving closer, he saw that the ground against the foundation had been disturbed, and a tiny wire extended upward about six inches from a mound of dirt beneath it. Duke had spotted it, as well, and was sniffing it cautiously, as if it might reach out and bite him. He growled softly as he backed away.

Leaning the shotgun against the house, Ben pulled some dirt away from what appeared to be an antenna of some kind. It was attached to a sphere about the size of a basketball, of a dull metallic makeup, with a blinking tiny red lamp on its side.

"Holy crap, Duke. What in the world is this?" Ben exclaimed. As if understanding what he had just asked, the dog slowly backed farther away, growling all the while. Ben backed away, too, trying to decide what to do next. It wasn't likely a bomb of some kind. The ones he had seen were usually cylindrical. A transmitter, maybe. Or receiver, or both. That would explain the antenna.

"I need to call Jim," he said to no one in particular.

Grabbing the shotgun and calling for Duke, he ran back to the kitchen door, went inside, and dialed Jim's number. After a couple of rings, a sleepy voice said, "Vickers."

"Jim, it's me, Ben. I need you to come to the house. Now." Ben was speaking in a little more than a whisper so as not to wake the women. Not likely they could hear him anyway, as they were on the other end of the house and upstairs.

Wide-awake now, Jim asked, "What happened? Is somebody hurt?"

"No, nothing like that," Ben replied. "I found something outside I need you to take a look at. And hurry, but no lights when you get close to the house. I'll meet you out front."

"On my way, buddy." He was already out of bed and moving quickly to get dressed as he hung up the phone.

The patrol car arrived within minutes, pulling into the driveway with only the outside security light illuminating it. Ben motioned for Jim to go with him to the back of the house, explaining what he had seen earlier. Flashlights in hand, they both bent down to examine the sphere.

"Well? What do you think? Ever see anything like this before?" Ben asked. He was hoping Jim would know exactly what it was.

"No, buddy. No idea. Don't think it's a bomb, though. I think it's some kind of receiver/transmitter thing. But I don't see a speaker or microphone anywhere. Have you tried to move it?" Jim looked at him anxiously.

"No. Haven't touched it," Ben assured him. "What do you think we ought to do with it?"

"Well, I think we need to get it away from the house. Anywhere." It was clear Jim didn't want to spend too much time with it.

"Yeah. How about we take it down to the Point? That's about as far away as I can think right now." Ben looked to Jim for his approval and got it in the form of a hearty nod.

Slowly Ben wiggled his fingers beneath the sphere until he was sure he could lift it. Then, bracing himself, he rose to his feet, the object cradled in his hands as delicately as he could. Jim had moved back about ten feet by now, his eyes wide.

"Hey, if this thing blows, you're going along with me, you know." Ben was half-laughing, his voice shaking a bit.

All Jim could say was "Come on, let's dump this thing before it does."

It seemed to take forever to cover the half mile or so to the point. Ben, stepping carefully into the light of Jim's flashlight, moved as quickly as he dared. Duke ran ahead and was waiting for them at the water's edge.

Ben gently set the sphere down onto the sand near some cattails. "This should be okay. The tide doesn't come up this far. Let's get out of here."

On the way back to the house, they puzzled over what they should do next. This was really weird, and they both agreed they had better be careful moving forward toward an answer. They would soon discover that this was only the beginning of more weird events that would change everything.

"Hey, Dave. Sorry to call at such an hour, but we need you over here at the house." Ben had decided that if anyone could figure this thing out, Dave could. After all, he did say once to call him if he needed anything.

"It's okay, I've been up all night anyway. Be right there."

That was easy, Ben thought. *Maybe we can get this all sorted out soon.*

Dave arrived less than fifteen minutes later, and he, Jim, and Ben crept down to the Point, where they had left the sphere. On the way, Ben filled Dave in on how all this came to be.

"Well, what do you think?" Ben asked, hoping for a quick, logical answer.

"Don't know," Dave whispered. "I'll have to take it with me."

"Really?" asked Jim. "Don't you think that might be dangerous?"

"Nah. Don't look dangerous." Dave was matter-of-fact about it, and it didn't seem to bother him at all.

"Okay," Ben stated. "But be careful."

Dave picked it up like he might pick up a basketball, tucked it under his arm, and they all went back to the house.

"I'll give you a call when I find out what this thing is," Dave said. Sounded like a done deal. Dave seemed to have no limits to his intellect, so his confidence was understandable.

Jim left soon after Dave, and Ben and Duke went inside to try to get some sleep for whatever was left of this night.

*****

Dave set the sphere on a small table in his office and stared at the object as he sipped a cup of coffee. He saw no identifying markings, no fasteners that held it together, nor did he see anything that revealed a power source, though the tiny red light shone brightly as before.

Like Ben, he figured the little antenna implied it was either a receiver, transmitter, or both. But where did its signal go or come from? That was the real puzzle. And it emitted no noise, at least none that he could discern. Weird. Really weird.

He glanced at the clock on his desk and saw that it was nearly five thirty. A quick look out the window revealed the sky getting lighter in the east. Getting sleepy all of a sudden, he leaned back in his office chair, put his feet on his desk, and closed his eyes. He didn't see the little red light begin to blink, turn green, then white. Nor did he see the faint glow surround the sphere as he slipped off to a deep, well-needed sleep.

*****

Ben woke to the sound of Aunt Louise calling softly from the kitchen. It was nearly seven o'clock, and both he and Duke had slept hard for the last couple of hours. Though he didn't feel like it, he got up and went downstairs, still wearing the jeans and T-shirt he'd slept in.

Aunt Louise already had coffee made, and its aroma mixed with that of bacon and eggs, which filled their plates. Olivia was at the table, with a glass of orange juice in her hand. She smiled and raised the glass as if to offer a toast to the morning.

"Good morning, everybody," Ben said as cheerily as he could.

Aunt Louise answered first, with a little more cheer than Ben had mustered.

With a mouth full of bacon, Olivia just grunted and nodded.

As Aunt Louise sat at the table, she asked Ben if he had heard any strange noises last night. Not sure what to say, he just mentioned that Jim had stopped by while he was on patrol and left after a short time. That seemed to satisfy her, and the conversation turned to small talk and then to the funeral the next day.

Ben realized that an extra plate had been set at the table and asked his aunt about it.

Smiling, Olivia answered quickly. "Jim is stopping by for breakfast, and then we're going into town. I need a couple things for tomorrow, and he graciously offered to take me. He's so sweet." Her smile gave her away, and Aunt Louise just shook her head. She knew the two of them were, in her words, "sweet on each other" and had been since the day they met years ago.

CHAPTER 4

Dave woke from his unexpected sleep to find himself in a strange room. Blinking back the surprise landscape, he discovered that he was, indeed, awake. Though his desk lay before him and his feet were still resting upon it, he was somewhere other than his workspace at home. The sphere still sat where he placed it, though the red light was now white.

The room was eerily quiet, well-lit, and as clean as a hospital operating room. Every surface was painted bright white and contained only a stainless steel sink on one wall. As he surveyed the room, he heard a door open behind him. He turned to see a tall man in a white lab coat, staring through the doorway at him. Because of the bright light behind the stranger, he couldn't make out any details that could describe him. The stranger looked at him with what appeared to be shock and disgust, quickly turning away and closing the door behind him.

Dave began to rise from his easy chair, and just as quickly, he was back home in his familiar office. Desk, chair, sphere—unmoved.

"Weird," he said aloud. He stood to his feet and walked around the room, touching everything to be sure the room was real. "I need to call Ben," he said to no one in particular.

*****

Duke ran to the kitchen door, barking as he went. Ben could see the distinctive lights of Jim's patrol car through the window, stopping in front of the house. Olivia got up from the table and beat Duke to the door, opened it, and all but sprinted to greet the sheriff as he got out of the car. Ben and Aunt Louise grinned as they watched the couple embrace as if they hadn't seen each other in years. Together they walked, hand in hand, toward the house.

After a few exchanges of "good mornings," they were off again to run some errands in town and, no doubt, spend some time catching up.

Aunt Louise grabbed the phone as it rang and passed it on to Ben. On the other end, Dave told him what had transpired at his home and said he'd be right over. He would call Jack and Jim, as well. He felt they needed to be there to discuss the strange event he had experienced. Ben told him he'd get hold of Jim later, withholding any reason. As he hung up, he told his aunt that the guys were stopping by soon but would hang out in the garage like they did in the old days. He didn't want to alarm her in any way and figured that would keep their meeting more private. She smiled and said that would be good for him and that she would prepare some light snacks for them. She then shooed him from the kitchen and, humming some happy tune, went about searching the cabinets for cookware and snack food.

*****

Deep in his watery enclave, the Boss was in a rage. He threw open doors and called his helpers to meet him in his office. "Now!" He was literally pulling at what little hair he had left when the most senior of his men entered the room. Though they had no idea what was going on or what had happened, they knew for sure that someone might not live through the day. They had witnessed this sort of rage in the past, and when it was over, there had been fewer of them than before. In those cases, distant screams could be heard, followed by the sound of splashing and gurgling just outside the main entrance to the structure. Then quiet. Afterward, the Boss wore a slight smile for a couple of days as their work resumed within the bowels of the rusting ship they called *The Cave*. Who would it be this time?

Still pacing behind his desk, the Boss placed both hands to his face in a failed attempt to calm himself. In almost a growl, he asked, "Who was the brilliant moron that placed the ball last night?" He took a deep breath and turned toward the small group of frightened men who stood before him. "Who was in charge of that?"

After only a few seconds, a balding short man sheepishly stepped forward. "I was," he all but whispered. "I had my best men on it, sir."

"Well then, I want you and your best men to report to the dock at sunset. In the meantime, turn your work over to your most competent supervisor. You will gather your best men and remain in your office until such time as you will be summoned to the dock. You will speak to no one. Is that understood?" The Boss's eyes shone like fire, piercing the very soul of the little man like a spear through Jell-O.

"Yes, sir. Permission to take my leave, sir?"

"Get out! All of you. Any more idiotic mistakes, and you'll all be snacks for the sharks. Now go, GO!"

It wasn't supposed to go that way last night. He had to find out what went wrong and who that clown who appeared in the sterile room was. He sat at his desk and pushed a button at the corner of his desk. Immediately a voice responded, "Yes, sir?"

"Get Sarah, and have her call me on the secure line. Now. Find her and tell her it's urgent." At this point, if she screwed up, she'd be fed to the sharks, as well, no matter what time of day. It might even be more pleasurable in the daylight to see better the fear on her face as she was devoured piece by piece before disappearing into the churning, blood-tinted dark water. That was an exciting thought. If not her, then he'd have to find someone else, now that the vision had entered his mind. Just the thought of it seemed to have a calming effect, making him almost giddy with anticipation. But there was work to do; he couldn't be distracted now.

*****

Ben stood in the garage, looking over the quiet scene before him. The cars sat neatly in place, ready for use. Everything in its place, all as if time had stopped until he was ready to set it in motion again. It was sad, really, to see everything at the ready, knowing that things wouldn't be the same. Not ever. As he began to feel a sense of being overwhelmed by it all, Aunt Louise entered.

"It's so good to see Olivia so happy. She speaks of Jim all the time, you know. And writes to him almost every day. I found a box of letters he had sent her over the past few years. I never read them, of course, and never mentioned them. I think they may have a future together. How about you, Ben? Do you have someone special?"

"Yeah, I do. I met her in Germany. She's a soldier too. We're very close. At least I think so. We've never really talked about us as being a couple, in that sense. But I plan to let her know, when I get back, just how I feel, I mean." There's an old saying about putting off until tomorrow what can be done today, and Ben wished he had followed that rule. Too late now, though.

"Well, I hope that if it is to be, it will be. I wish only the best for you, as I do Olivia. Sometimes, destiny can be difficult to understand. We must look for the path forward and let, in this case, love reveal itself. It cannot be rushed or created. It's there and will pour itself over you in time." Aunt Louise was mysterious at times but right almost always.

She hugged Ben and returned to the kitchen just as Dave and Jack pulled up to the open garage door.

Without even saying hello, Dave went into the events of the night. He went on to theorize that the device they had found was responsible; that was clear. It was some kind of "transport" device and one that could move things through time. He had noticed that his wall clock had not moved when he found himself back in his office but that everything had returned to normal once there. In his words, "it's a really cool thing," and he wanted to inspect it further.

Ben and Jack realized how dangerous that would be, given there was no way to know when it might activate again nor where he would end up.

"That thing was meant for you, my friend. It was just luck that it wasn't here when it woke up." Dave was serious, and they all knew he was right.

"Well, what do we do with it, then? Whoever put it there is going to want it back or try again when we least expect it." Jack looked back and forth at his friends as he spoke.

"You're the genius, Dave. What do you think?" Ben asked.

"I've got a place where I can put it. And I've got these neat cameras and audio I can monitor it with. Unless they can vary the intensity of it, to move more stuff, it'll be safely away from anything it could harm. I might even be able to put a tracking device on it just in case it goes somewhere again, and maybe a message." Smart as he was, Dave was also a practical joker who loved creating funny, if not extremely confusing, scenarios to get the best of his friends. And sometimes, for people he didn't particularly like. He was good at it and never revealed his methods nor who might have set the jokes up.

It was agreed that Dave's idea was best for now and that they had all best stay vigilant. They had no idea who was behind this or why, so they would pair up to watch each other's back. Might take some explaining, but there was a lot at stake here. And perhaps most importantly, this would stay among only the four of them. It was far too strange to share with anyone outside their circle.

As they finished their discussion, Aunt Louise entered with scrambled eggs, scrapple, toast, cinnamon buns, coffee, orange juice, fresh fruit, and enough plates for everyone.

"You're the best, Aunt Louise," said Dave.

They all thanked her as she smiled and went back into the house.

*****

When breakfast was over, Dave and Jack left after agreeing they would pair up to cover each other. Jack wasn't crazy about being anywhere near that metal ball, but he trusted Dave to do the right thing. If there was anybody who could sort that thing out, it was Dave. Ben would fill Jim in when he returned and come up with a plan to ensure they could stick close together until this mess was over. The biggest hurdle in that respect would be Olivia. She sure wouldn't mind Jim being around, but having to share him with Ben could be a problem. They'd work it out, though.

Entering the kitchen, Ben thanked Aunt Louise again for the breakfast she had prepared for the guys. As she cleaned up the dishes, Ben excused himself, going up to his room, Duke at his side. He figured he'd get his uniform ready for tomorrow, polish up his shoes, and get some rest later.

Aunt Louise was soon busying herself around the house as Ben finished up his tasks. He and Duke went outside, planning a walk through the field and back to the Point. It was a beautiful day, and he had some thinking to do. Mostly about Allie, though the sphere kept interfering with more pleasant thoughts. Duke was running ahead, returning occasionally to Ben's side as if to hurry him along. After a while, they both reached the small beach at the Point and sat together, looking out over the water. It was peaceful, with only a couple of boats offshore, moving slowly as the skippers worked their lines, hauling in crabs for some lucky person's dinner. Another small skiff, occupied by two men, sat farther away. One of the men had binoculars to his eyes, lowering them quickly as Ben watched. With no sound, just like the small boat he had seen the other night, they motored away and around the far shoreline.

Coincidence? Ben thought. *Don't think so.*

"Come on, Duke. Let's get back to the house."

As he stood to leave, the sound of another boat close by caught his attention. "Aw, crap, not her."

"Hi, Ben. Help me in." It was Sarah.

"Don't you ever work?" Ben replied as she cut the motor and tossed a rope his way.

"Sure. But I get to set my own hours most of the time. Perk of the job." She hopped out of the skiff and ran her fingers through her hair. "I was passing by and saw you here. Thought I'd stop and say hi."

"Hello. Duke and I were just heading back to the house. I've got a lot of stuff to do before tomorrow."

"Oh yeah. The funeral is tomorrow. I'm so sorry, Ben. I plan to be there for you. I know it's going to be difficult. I want to be here for you while you're home, so expect to see me often." She gave Ben those sad "puppy" eyes she was so adept at.

"Thanks, but we're pretty squared away. Maybe I'll call you if I need anything." *Not hardly*, he thought. She would only bring grief and fake sympathy to the situation. Some people bought into it, but not anyone he knew. She always wanted something to meet her own needs and nothing more.

"Well, we gotta go. Maybe I'll see you tomorrow." Ben turned to leave, but she moved to his side.

"Just wondering. You finding out anything about what happened to your parents? I mean, like how? Some people are asking, that's all."

"No. Haven't really taken the time yet. Maybe we'll have answers down the road." She sure was being pushy, he thought.

"Maybe I can stop by this weekend. I'd like to know more about your father. And your mom, too, of course. What kind of stuff he did in the service. You know, just to know more about him. Them."

"Yeah, maybe. Just read the obituaries. That'll tell you enough." A little agitated, Ben turned, and with Duke close at his side, they headed back to the house. The small boat with the two men watching him, now Sarah showing up at the point. Coincidence? Maybe. But with everything that had happened lately, he couldn't be sure. Sarah wouldn't even look his way when they were in school. *She wants something. And working for Mr. Sterling, I'm sure she nosed around and probably knows*

*more about his inheritance than he does. She can smell money a mile
away, so that's a possibility.*

Jim and Olivia returned later in the afternoon, clearly enjoying
themselves as they spent some alone time together. Aunt
Louise went to her room to prepare for tomorrow, and Ben
joined the couple on the dock for a cup of coffee and a danish.

After some small talk, Ben told Jim he needed to talk some
"business" with him. They excused themselves and left Duke
watching over Olivia on the dock. They went into the garage,
and Ben told him about Dave's experience. Jim agreed with
their plan to stick close together for the time being, and they
came up with a way to make that happen. Ben would tell Olivia
and Louise that he needed Jim close by for the next couple
of days. They would understand and agree without question.
Olivia certainly wouldn't mind.

Later, at the kitchen table, they revealed their plan and, as
expected, were met with agreement. Olivia, though trying to be
somber, barely held her excitement that Jim would be staying
for a while. He would take up residence in the downstairs
bedroom, next to the garage. So it was set.

They all talked into the night, covering the schedule for
tomorrow and speculating on what would follow in the coming
days. Duke watched intently as if he understood it all. Maybe
he did. After all, strange things were happening lately.

Later, everyone went to bed in their respective rooms, Duke
following Ben to their room. After everyone had settled down,
Ben and Duke took the first watch, hoping the night would
be a quiet one. Later, Jim would position himself in a spot
where he could keep watch, joined by Duke, as well. Tomorrow
would be a long day, and everyone needed to get as much rest
as they could.

After his watch, Ben left Duke with Jim and went to bed, where sleep quickly found him. His dreams were filled with men in boats, rooms full of spheres bouncing from wall to wall, and Allie. Though dreams of Allie were commonplace, filled with a joy that allowed him to wake with a smile, tonight her appearance brought on a sadness, the reason for which he could not discern.

Meanwhile, at Dave's house, he and Jack were enjoying a glass of red wine. The living room was only dimly lit with a single small lamp as they sipped their drinks and recalled the events of the day.

The sudden sound of splintering wood and the crash of the back door hitting the floor shook them enough that their wineglasses hit the floor almost simultaneously, breaking into tiny shards and splashing wine everywhere.

Almost as suddenly, Jack was on his feet, moving toward the sound as two men entered the room. Dressed in black, they moved quickly toward Jack and Dave, as if they had rehearsed this attack. And though they moved with speed, they seemed to move laboriously, as if all their appendages were struggling to work properly.

Dave ducked just as the first attacker swung an unusually long arm toward his head, the momentum briefly throwing him off balance. Dave took the opportunity to lunge at his opponent's feet, further impairing his attempt to strike him with the extended arm. As Dave grabbed his two legs with both arms, he twisted to one side, and the man fell heavily to the floor. Taking up a large splinter that was only seconds before a doorframe, he thrust it into his attacker's thigh, resulting in a painful groan and significant spilling of blood.

Dave could see then that his attacker had what appeared to be a metal arm. Should he strike a good blow with it, the fight would be over. Dave rolled away, jumped to his feet, and landed a solid kick to the metal man's head. Though it hurt his bare foot significantly, it did the job and put an end to the scuffle.

As Dave turned from his defeated battle partner, he saw Jack kick his opponent square in the face after having, just seconds before, placed a well-aimed kick to his groin. For just a moment, there was relative silence in the room, save for soft whimpering by their uninvited guests. Dave took the opportunity to reach into a drawer in a nearby side table and pull out a .45-caliber semiautomatic he kept there for "special occasions." This occasion seemed special enough.

Jack ordered the two intruders to sit against the wall while Dave held the pistol on them. Slowly the two crawled to their spots, groaning and holding various parts of their bodies to ease the pain that had been inflicted upon them.

"Who are you?" Jack insisted. "Why are you here?"

CHAPTER 5

Ben reached out to shut off his alarm clock: 6:00 a.m. Still groggy from a restless night, he looked out the window to be greeted by a gray sky. "Oh, great," he said to himself. "Now it's going to be even gloomier today."

After a shower, he dressed and went down to the kitchen. Aunt Louise was already at work, preparing breakfast and much-needed coffee. She turned and smiled at Ben as he entered and, without a word, set a plate on the table for him. She had prepared his favorites: scrambled eggs, scrapple, toast, and a glass of cold milk.

"Have some coffee, and I'll get Olivia and Jim," she said. "They'll want something to eat too."

She soon returned with the pair following behind. Both appeared fully awake and were holding hands as they went to the table. Jim sat down, and Olivia moved to the counter to help her mother take more food to them.

"How you doin' this morning?" asked Jim.

"Okay, I guess. I'll know more after a cup of coffee," Ben replied as he sipped the much-needed brew. "I'll just be glad when this day is over." This was a day Ben dreaded most. It would place a sense of finality on everything he knew as recently as a week before. There was no redo, no chance to change the outcome of where he found himself. Everything would be different now, and there was nothing anyone could do about it. Might as well get the day over with and decide how to move on.

The phone rang, and Aunt Louise answered it.

"It's for you, Ben. It's your friend Dave," she said as she handed him the phone.

"Hey, buddy. How are you this morning?" Ben asked in the cheeriest voice he could muster.

"We're coming over, and we've got a story to tell. Be there in a few minutes." He hung up before Ben could even ask what it was all about.

*****

After Dave and Jack arrived, the four friends, and Duke, went to the garage to get updated on the events at Dave's house the night before. Jim and Ben could only listen in disbelief as Dave shared the details of what had happened.

After the two thugs had been subdued, it became apparent they were not your normal home invaders. The one with unusually long arms was deformed in other ways, as well.

One leg was partially metal and ended in an artificial foot, painted to look like a shoe. The other man appeared to be normal, except for a mechanical hand that seemed to be flawlessly connected to his wrist. While it was clear from their physical attributes, combined with their size and physique, that they could have easily overcome Ben's friends, it seemed their hearts just weren't in it.

They confessed that they had been sent to find a device that was tracked to the house and told to eliminate anyone who was present. While they were simply following orders from someone they called the Boss, they discovered that when it came time to carry out those orders, they just weren't prepared to go that far. The smaller of the two did admit that if they could have killed the pair immediately upon entering the house, that would have been okay. They just weren't in for a prolonged fight with such fierce opposition.

They told of how their physical abnormalities had been the result of some experiments carried out at the Boss's orders, leaving them joined to some nearby metal structure they happened to be in contact with. They were still alive only because of some careful, skilled surgery that left them in their present state. Because of threats to them and their families, they were left to carry out various tasks for the Boss and his henchmen. They were told their families thought they were dead, and they wouldn't fit into society anyway because of their conditions. Tired of being treated like the freaks they were, they, and several others like them, were trying to figure out a way to get in touch with their families and escape this prison, or "zoo," as they referred to it.

The device they were looking for was some kind of time/molecular transformation device the Boss was working on. That was all they knew, except that it was dangerous and was one of a dozen or so kept in a secure location offshore. While they weren't sure of the Boss's motives, they had overheard talk that no good would come from his success. He was clearly a madman and a dangerous one at that. More than one member of his staff and crew had disappeared without a trace, some simply for disagreeing with him on a path forward to completing his plan.

Dave had asked if they had anything to do with the death of Ben's parents. They did not; however, they suspected the Boss was responsible in some way. They had heard that someone was too close to discovering his plan, as well as the location of his "office," referring to the offshore enclave.

Since Jack and Dave didn't know what to do with them, they ordered them from the house with the promise they'd be shot dead next time they came around. And not just to his house, but near any of their friends', as well. Reluctantly, the two "iron men" left through what was left of the door. Unable to return to the zoo after having botched the mission, they would find someplace to hide until they could figure out what to do. Against his better judgment, Dave gave them directions to a small weekend house his late father had built near the bay. They would find food and shelter there, and no one ever went near the place. That should give them some time to get themselves sorted out. Dave threw a small first aid kit at them and told them to get moving.

As they left, the larger of the two turned to Dave and said, "If you run into more trouble because of this, you'll know where to find us. We can help, and I know there are others that will help too. The Boss will eliminate anybody and anything that gets in his way. If things get rough, you won't be able to handle it yourselves. His influence goes way up to the top. Law enforcement, military, you name it. And he knows people, so trust nobody. And I mean *no body*. Thanks for not shooting us. We owe you." With that, he turned and, with his partner, walked into the early-morning shadows.

As Jack finished his story, the garage fell silent. There were questions that needed to be answered and action that needed to be taken, but right now, they were stunned.

Jack broke the silence in his sometimes-deadpan way. "I would have shot them."

Dave spoke up. "The Philadelphia Experiment," he stated.

Everyone looked at him.

Ben said to no one in particular, "I've heard my dad talk about that. Wasn't that a myth or something, about a navy ship disappearing, crew members dying, going crazy, melting into the ship's superstructure?"

"Exactly," Dave answered. "I think that's exactly what's going on here. They say it is a myth or conspiracy theory, but the facts bear it out as a true incident. Some say the ship disappeared from its dock in Philly and reappeared briefly in Norfolk. Even Einstein and Tesla were involved early on, but the navy got hold of it. Then it all went wrong, so they shut it down, or at least they said they did. The experiment was abandoned by the military, and I think someone has taken it over. Why, I have no idea, but it can't be good."

They agreed to keep this information to themselves for the time being and get on with the day's business. No need to alarm Louise and Olivia or anyone else. The day was going to be a busy one, and they could talk about it later, but for now, best to let it go.

CHAPTER 6

The funeral had gone on for what seemed like hours. The church was crowded with people, only a few of whom Ben knew. Mostly civilians, there were many attendees in uniform, from high-ranking noncommissioned officers to a couple of Generals. Under normal circumstances, that would have made him uncomfortable to be around such high-level people, but today, he had other things on his mind. He wished Allie were here. She always made him feel at ease, no matter the circumstance.

Aunt Louise and Olivia shed many a tear during the service, as did a few others Ben could see. The preacher said many kind words about his parents and tried his best to offer comfort to everyone. When he was finished with the service, he invited everyone to the cemetery for the interment, after which a dinner and get-together would be available in the church fellowship hall. Though he had no desire to go, Ben felt it would be best to be present, if even for a short while.

At the cemetery, full military honors were rendered, and Ben was presented with the traditional folded flag. Then it was back to the church to formally meet some of those who attended the services. He stayed close to Aunt Louise and Olivia, as did Jim. Soon, Jim and Olivia sat together in the back of the hall, Jim with his arm around her as they talked. Aunt Louise spoke to many others as she eventually made her way around, greeting old friends and accepting condolences from them.

Ben did the same, discovering that most of the uniformed men and women had worked with his father, some closely on projects they couldn't reveal. Some of the civilians turned out to be from the Department of Defense and the Pentagon. They were truly stunned when they heard of the accident. His dad's work, even after he had officially retired, had been an important part of national security and would leave a void in their operations. This revelation surprised him as he thought his dad had left all that behind. Something to think about, for sure.

As he pondered his dad's work, a Major General approached him with an extended hand.

"Sergeant Dawson, I'm General Briggs, and this is Sergeant Major Hammer. We admired your folks and worked with your father for many years at the department. He'll be missed."

Ben shook their hands and thanked them for coming. The Sergeant Major summoned up what looked to be a smile, but Ben could tell that wasn't something he did often. His demeanor was all business.

General Briggs spoke first. "At some point, soon, we'll need to talk with you. I'll be in touch, but meanwhile, if there's anything you need, call me on my direct line. Here's my card. Safeguard it. I'll confess, we have watched your career progression closely and can see a lot of your father in you. You are to be commended. Ever thought about going into the officer corps?"

"I think you'd better serve your country as an NCO." Sergeant Major Hammer gave him a wink and nudged the General. It was obvious these two had a good relationship.

"I plan to apply for Warrant Officer, Sergeant Major. Dad supported that decision, as well. He thought it would suit me. He always said I favored a 'hands-on' approach to everything."

"Well, if you change your mind, I'm sure you'll do well." The General pulled him aside and got more serious for a moment. "Let me be clear on something, Sergeant. Given the circumstances of your parents' deaths, we launched our investigation. There's more to it than has been reported. And given the work your father was involved in, we believe there is a national security component at play. Don't speak to anyone about this, and trust no one. If you have any questions in the coming days, contact me or the Sergeant Major. His number is on the card, as well. Say nothing on the phone. We'll be in touch and set up a meeting. Understand?"

"Yes, sir. There are a few things I need to tell you about, and a couple close friends are already involved."

"We know who they are. They've been checked out. They need to know that anything that happens must remain among yourselves and reported to us immediately. Speak only to me and Sergeant Major Hammer. No one else. That's vital. We clear?" The General was dead serious.

"Yes, sir." Ben was really confused now and wanted some answers too. So at least he and his buddies had a couple of allies in high places. "We'll need to give you some information on some stuff that's been happening the past couple days. We should meet soon."

"We'll be in touch." They shook Ben's hand once more and excused themselves from the hall.

Ben had to restrain himself from gathering up his buddies and relaying this information to them right now. There were still people to meet and formalities to attend to. So for the time being, he had to get on with business and get the day over with. After checking on Aunt Louise and Olivia, he made his way over to Dave and Jack, who were heavily engaged in conversation with a couple of young women. He whispered to them that they would need to meet later this evening in the garage that had somehow become their conference room. They both nodded, so Ben left them to whatever it was the ladies found so fascinating.

Just when he thought things were winding down, Sarah appeared in front of him. Inside, he was hoping he wouldn't run into her, though he also knew it would be unavoidable. There were many of his old school friends here today, and he enjoyed seeing them, in spite of the circumstances. This was one, however, he could do without. Especially today.

"I'm so sorry, Ben," she said with fake sincerity. Everyone knew she was incapable of compassion. But she could pour it on when she wanted, or needed, to. Most could see through her expert acting, but some succumbed to her before experiencing her true personality. And it usually ended up tragically or, at the very least, emotionally devastating.

"Thank you. And thanks for coming." Ben hated lying, even to someone like her. He didn't plan on being too cordial today. She couldn't be trusted in any way. His guard was up, and the sooner he could remove himself from her, the better.

"If you don't mind, I'd like to come by the house later. Bring some food for you all."

"Well, the church is preparing a bunch of stuff for us to take home, but thanks for the offer." That should take care of that, he figured.

"No trouble at all," she said. "I've already got it ready. Some of your favorite foods. I'll see you later." And with a kiss on his cheek, she turned and walked away with no time to debate. Before walking out the door, she turned and gave that silly little wave she always did. Probably had to decide on which untraceable poison to put in the food, he thought. And how did she know what his favorite foods were?

Later, on the drive home, everyone was quiet. Olivia rode with Jim, and Jack rode with Dave. They said they'd come by later but had some things to attend to. Probably those two women they were talking to earlier. Aunt Louise said little on the short trip, and Ben assumed she felt the same as he did. Over, done, no turning back the clock and changing outcomes. What to do from here. There would be time to get their lives back in order and figure out how to handle the days and weeks to come. No need to rush. But Ben knew it wasn't going to be easy for any of them. And she and Olivia didn't even know what was going on after dark. All this crazy stuff was going to be hard to hide, but it had to be done. Besides, he had no desire to get on the bad side of General Briggs or Sergeant Major Hammer. That would likely not go well.

Later, back at the house, Ben sat at the kitchen table with Duke close by on the floor. He seemed to discern Ben's sadness, and as the dog rested his head on his master's foot, he let out a sigh before closing his eyes. Duke was usually full of energy, especially after being left alone for a time. He would run around the yard when Ben let him out and try to play when they went back in. But not today. Duke was a perceptive animal, almost exhibiting human characteristics at times. So Ben wasn't at all surprised at how he was acting now.

"There is much to do now, isn't there? Don't you have to return to your unit soon?" Louise was making coffee and putting away the food the church sent home with them.

"Yeah. I've got another week or so before I have to get back. More time if I need it. I think I can wrap things up here, though. Mr. Sterling already has some paperwork done. All I have to do is sign some stuff, and I can get into the details later. What about you and Olivia? Maybe you could stay on here for a while? That's a lot to ask, but I'm sure Mom would have liked to see you stay a while and watch over things until we can come up with something." Ben found himself almost begging her to stay, but knew she had a home to go to and her own life back in Belgium.

"That's sweet of you, Ben. I'll speak to Olivia about it. She's always loved it here, and I suspect more so since Jim's around. We'll see."

"Thanks. You know the house is yours for as long as you want. I expect to be in the Army another fifteen or more years, so there's that to consider. Selling the property is out of the question. But I won't press you on it. I'll respect your decision." And he would. Maybe someday he'd come back here to stay, but that was a long way off. Besides, if everything went as planned with Allie, she might want to live somewhere else. One thing at a time.

By early evening, Jim had returned with Olivia, and Jack and Dave were mulling about in the garage, no doubt bragging about the two women they had met earlier. Ben and Jim joined them, and they made themselves comfortable in some lawn chairs that had been stored against one wall. It was time to share the conversation Ben had with the General and the Sergeant Major. They each swore to secrecy the information and activities of the last twenty-four hours and discussed how to assess their predicament. The most surprising information was when Jim shared his discovery of the dark sedan that always seemed to be in the area, usually wherever Ben happened to be. He confessed that after his second sighting of the mysterious car, he also kept an eye on Ben. He struggled with confronting the passengers or just watching from a distance but wasn't sure if they were good guys or bad guys. Their government license plate turned up nothing out of the ordinary, so he felt it best to just let it ride for a while. After all, they had made no aggressive moves, so far.

So now there was an added element to the strange events that had taken place lately, and they were certain everything was connected. As they discussed the possible links and reasons all this might be happening, a soft knock on the garage door caused them to stop talking altogether.

"Ben?" said Aunt Louise. "Someone here to see you."

"Okay, be right there," Ben answered. *Has to be Sarah*, he thought. He was hoping she had changed her mind about coming over.

As he entered the living room, Duke at his side, she gave him a smile and approached him with her arms outstretched. She stopped abruptly, however, when Duke leaned forward and met her with a deep growl.

"It's okay, Duke. Relax." Ben said. "Sorry, he's pretty protective lately. Have a seat."

She looked puzzled. "Why? Anything going on lately that would make him act that way?"

"No," Ben stated. "He's just a little out of sorts with all that's happened the last couple weeks. He's pretty perceptive, you know." Perceptive, alright. He knew all he needed to know about Sarah, better than most people did.

"I brought a few goodies for you all, just snacks and things," she said as she motioned toward the kitchen. "So what's your plan now? You going back overseas now, or are you staying around awhile?"

"Not sure yet. Still have a few days to take care of business. Lots of paperwork to do. We'll see." She was being her nosy self, which wasn't surprising. The less she knew, the better, and Ben figured he'd put her on top of his new "don't trust anyone" list. He had a feeling the list would grow before all this was over, but she would likely remain high up in a place of dubious honor.

"I'll keep you posted if there's anything you might need to know. Sorry, I have to go now. Got a couple friends over."

"Oh yeah. Jack, Dave, and Jim. You guys have been close since high school, haven't you?"

Ben took her statement to be more than just small talk. Her tone was as if she wanted him to know that she knew who was here. Jim and Dave were easy to figure out since their cars were out front. But Jack rode with Dave, so it had to be a guess, though an easy one.

"Well, I'll go now. Nice seeing you, just sorry about the circumstances. We'll get together before you leave. I'd really like to spend some time with you." She moved to hug Ben but checked herself and looked at Duke. Though he watched her closely, he remained quiet, as if daring her to move another inch closer. Ben said nothing, thankful that the dog intervened.

"Sure. Maybe I'll call you." Or maybe not.

"Aunt Louise will see you out. Thanks again for coming over." With a quiet sigh of relief, Ben rubbed Duke's head in thanks, and they returned to the garage.

"Okay, guys, here's the deal. Remember, trust no one. And Sarah is at the top of the list. Try to avoid her if you can." That should be to the point, Ben thought. From here on out, life might get just a little difficult.

He turned to Dave. "Tomorrow we go see those two guys that visited you last night. Maybe they can answer some questions. I have to wonder now if the disappearances Jim mentioned are related to all this. He can fill you guys in on that," he said as he saw the puzzled look on Jack's and Dave's faces. "Let's meet at Dave's house around ten. You guys okay with that?"

They all nodded and began filing out of the garage and toward the kitchen. There, Louise was clearing off the counter and putting away the snacks Sarah had brought with her.

They all said their "good nights" and left. Ben thanked Aunt Louise for all she had done and excused himself. He would need a good night's sleep, if that was possible. Tomorrow could turn out to be a busy day, sprinkled with some surprises, and if they were lucky, some answers to the growing number of questions Ben had.

It didn't take Ben long to drift into a fitful sleep, with Duke lying quietly beside the bed.

Outside, hidden in the shadows near the shoreline, two pairs of eyes watched as, one by one, the lights were turned off in the big house.

CHAPTER 7

In a small valley within sight of the Bavarian Alps lay the small town of Walchensee. Sharing the valley was a crystal-clear lake, fed by the many mountain streams nearby, as well as snowmelt that occurred each spring. This time of year, the hills at the foot of the mountains were turning green, spotted with grazing cows and sheep. It was like looking at a postcard in each direction. Bavarian chalets on the hillside, bales of straw and hay harvested the previous fall were spread throughout the pastures, and here and there was a crudely built small shed housing tools or even a small tractor.

Ben had asked Allie to accompany him here for the weekend to share the serene beauty of this village he had only discovered a few months before. She agreed and was eager to see what Ben had described as one of the most beautiful places he had ever seen.

As they rounded the last corner of the mountain road Ben's Volkswagen had struggled to ascend, Walchensee lay below them, the lake shimmering in the midmorning sun. He glanced over to see her eyes grow wide as she took in the scene below. "It's beautiful" was all she said, as if the view had taken her breath away. Her gaze was fixed on what lay before them.

"Told you. We'll get a room at a Gasthaus and then take a rowboat out onto the lake. That be okay?"

"Sure," she replied as she turned to look at him with a smile.

After getting a room and driving over to the lake, they were soon lazily moving across the still water, taking in the scenery. Everywhere they looked, they found another scene that was breathtaking. But in spite of all the beauty that surrounded them, Ben couldn't take his eyes off Allie. She was far more interesting to look at than even the majestic Alps in the distance.

On the spur of the moment, he reached into the neckline of his shirt and pulled out his dog tags. While he was required, as every soldier was, to wear the Army-issued tags around the clock, some soldiers removed them while off duty. Ben always wore his, as it just didn't feel right to be without them. One tag was attached directly to the chain that hung around his neck, while the identical second tag hung from a smaller chain to the main one. On each tag was his name, service number, religious preference, and blood type.

As he removed the smaller chain and tag, he asked Allie for hers. Without question, she pulled her chain out and removed her tag.

"Do you keep a spare?" he asked.

"Sure do. I assume a good Sergeant like you always has a spare as well."

"Yes, I do," he replied, smiling.

After they exchanged their tags, she tilted her head to the side and, with a sly smile, asked, "Does this mean we're going steady?"

"Yeah. If that's okay with you."

"Yes. Yes, it is." She leaned forward and gave him a kiss. Without tucking the attached tag back into her blouse, she turned to look out at the landscape, clutching the new tag tightly, and smiled.

*****

A gentle rain welcomed the dawn as Ben stirred fitfully in his bed. With thoughts and visions of Allie still in his head, mingling with the reality of where he was, he quickly threw the bedcovers away and practically jumped from the bed. Even Duke was startled by Ben's rapid exit. He stared at his friend, unsure of what to do next, so he just watched closely as Ben stepped to the window and stared outside, holding tightly to the dog tags that hung around his neck. He opened his hand and read the tag that he held: "Morgan, Allie F." He shook his head as he realized he didn't even know what the *F* stood for. Another one of those "There's always tomorrow" moments.

"I've got to get things wrapped up here and get back to my unit," he said to himself. What he really meant was that he had to see Allie. Not just in a dream, but in person, for real. He wanted to touch her, feel her heartbeat as they held each other close.

"Okay, Duke. Today we get moving and start putting an end to this crazy circus, one way or another. I'll get whatever papers Mr. Sterling has and sign what I need to, call General Briggs and fill him in so he can do his thing, and convince Aunt Louise that she and Olivia should stay here. You can help take care of them till I get back stateside. Right, buddy?"

Duke seemed to understand and barked his acceptance of the duty that lay ahead. "Okay, let's get moving."

Ben got dressed and descended the stairs with his newfound enthusiasm, Duke close behind. As usual, Aunt Louise was preparing breakfast and greeted them both with a smile.

"I was just about to call for you two. Ready for breakfast? Your coffee is ready to pour."

"Thanks, Aunt Louise. Let me get Duke outside, and I'll be ready."

As Ben opened the door to let Duke run outside, the phone rang, taking Ben and Duke by surprise. Ben grabbed it, suspecting another crisis had developed overnight.

"This Sergeant Dawson?" the voice asked. It was clearly General Briggs. "Yes, it is." Catching him off guard, Ben didn't know what to say.

"Be at the Smith Island lighthouse at 0930. You know where that is. And I know your dad's boat is prepared for the trip. It always is. Come alone, and don't tell anyone where you're going." The General was abrupt and to the point, and he didn't leave any time for questions. Ben had no choice but to believe he was serious and that what he had in mind was something important.

"I'll see you there." With that, he hung up.

Ben found Jim in the garage and simply told him he had to go out for a couple of hours. Jim tried to ask what it was all about, but Ben was able to convince him he just needed some time to think and that he would be back as soon as he could. He grabbed the key to the *Catalina* from the box on the garage wall and went back into the kitchen.

"Going for a boat ride, Aunt Louise. Jim will be here if you need anything. Duke will be with me."

Before Aunt Louise could say anything, he was out the door, calling for Duke, and together they went to the dock, untied the boat, and jumped in. It started perfectly, and checking the gauges, he backed away.

Slowly idling down the creek, Ben scanned the gauges once more and throttled up, Duke hanging his head out the side to catch the familiar salt breeze and spray as the boat gained speed.

Ben tried to imagine what might be so urgent that he had to meet the General so soon and in such a desolate place. Maybe they were being watched or followed everywhere. That thought prompted Ben to look behind. All he saw were a couple of crabbers far off, working their lines, and a small skiff with two men aboard. They had no fishing or crabbing gear onboard that he could see and seemed to be trying futilely to keep up with the pair in the speeding *Catalina*. Ben made note of that, although it was probably nothing to be concerned about. There was no way they could keep up, and he would lose them long before he reached the bay.

In spite of the urgency and mystery surrounding this trip and all that had transpired up till now, Ben enjoyed the ride. Now and then, a bit of spray would splash past him, and he could recall the familiar smell of home. Salt water, the swamp milkweed, woodreeds—all painted a picture of better times. Though he longed for those days, he still missed Allie most of all. Where was she? What was she doing? Did she know where he was? And why was he called away so hastily? He would have time to sort all that out soon, he hoped. Right now, there were things that needed tending to before he could get back to his unit and Allie.

*****

At the house, the phone rang, and Aunt Louise answered it as Jim and Olivia entered the kitchen. Handing the phone to Jim, she said, "It's for you. Your friend Dave, I think."

"Thank you. How 'bout I take it in the living room. Shouldn't take long."

Aunt Louise nodded as she pressed the hold button with one finger and turned a couple of eggs over in the frying pan with the spatula she held in the other hand. "Don't be long, or you breakfast will get cold."

"I won't," he said as he turned to wink at a smiling Olivia.

"What's up, buddy? Ben's not here," he said softly into the phone. Dave sounded excited. "That's okay. Listen, I believe I was right about that sphere thing. I've had time to think about what happened to me. Somehow, someone has developed a small-scale version of what was tried with the Philadelphia Experiment. Only whoever it is can target their subjects more precisely and even move them back and forth. And move them through time. For me, it was only a couple minutes, based on my wall clock, and I don't know yet if that can be manipulated, as well."

"What did you do with it? Is it still with you?" Jim was genuinely concerned.

"Heck no. I've moved it far enough away, I think. Based on what appeared to move with me when that thing activated. I can tell you, though, that if they activate it again, they're going to be in for a surprise."

As he chuckled he said, "I'll say no more, but they'll sure have a mess on their hands."

"I'll take your word for it. Look, soon as Ben gets back, we'll call you and Jack. We have to get together and figure out what's going on. Ben has to get back to Germany, and I don't know how much leave he has left. Gotta go. You'll hear from us soon."

Jim hung up and went back to the kitchen. Aunt Louise gave him a concerned glance then served up breakfast as Olivia set coffee and toast on the table.

Hope nobody asks any questions, Jim thought to himself.

Soon they were chatting away, though, as if everything were normal. Jim quickly felt more at ease as the ate a pleasant breakfast.

*****

In his office offshore, the Boss sat, fuming over the arrival of a stranger into the secret place some called the Zoo. He pressed a button on his desk and summoned the new chief of operations. "My office. Now!" he shouted.

*****

Soon, a soft knock on the door told him the chief was outside. "Enter," the Boss said, with the irritation in his voice coming across very clearly. The chief had barely closed the door behind him, when the Boss said, "Send for the transport ball, and have it arrive here in my office. I want to check for damage or tampering. If anyone comes with it, eliminate them immediately. Now go. Then be here when it arrives."

"Yes, sir," the chief said as he hurried from the room. In just a few minutes, he returned and stood in a far corner, a large-caliber firearm in his hand, aimed at the center of the room. His hand shook visibly in anticipation of what might materialize in a few seconds.

The smell of ozone filled the air as the center of the room became blurry. In an instant, they could make out the sphere, accompanied by something else. The smell of ozone gave way to the unmistakable smell of salt water and rotting seaweed. Then crabs, hundreds of crabs. The rotted wooden cage that held them all broke apart and spread across the room along with gallons of dirty seawater. Crabs of all sizes scampered around, some washed across the floor as the water, no longer contained, washed over the expensive carpet, under their feet, and quickly covered every corner of the room. As the Boss picked up his feet, his chair fell back, and he soon lay on the floor with the crabs, trying to pick away the seaweed.

The chief stood as still as a statue, surprised at what the sphere brought back and knowing that he likely wouldn't live to see tomorrow. So he did what he thought might be his best chance at survival. Dropping the gun, he ran, slipped, slid to the door, exited, and ran down the hall toward the main entrance of the Zoo. Struggling, he opened the rusty door and jumped into the murky water, hoping the sharks only came around at night, when the Boss usually fed incompetent staff to them. He swam for his life. The shoreline sure looked a long way off.

Making a sandwich as he looked out his kitchen window overlooking the small dock where he kept his crab pots and cages, just in time, Dave watched as the sphere, along with his crab stash and hundreds of gallons of water, grew fuzzy then disappeared altogether. Smiling, he spread a little jelly on top of the peanut butter, poured a glass of milk, and enjoyed his morning meal.

*****

Ben steered the boat from the bay toward the Choptank River. The cruise had been pleasant, bringing back pleasant memories of the days not so long ago when his dad had allowed him to captain the boat on their many excursions to Cambridge, a little farther up the river. So many times they had come up here to watch the fireworks from offshore near Long Wharf then motor lazily back home in the calm waters of the rivers and bay. Other trips here would include fishing for stripers, or rock, as they were sometimes called. He could never forget the excitement of reeling in a large striper, Mom and Dad looking on and encouraging him. Today, unfortunately, was not such a day.

As the lighthouse came into view, Ben slowed to a near idle and looked around. The lighthouse was little more than a metal skeleton structure with a light on top, about twenty-five feet from the water's surface. It served merely as a marker to local watermen and as a cautionary method to keep them off the shallows behind it.

In the distance were a couple of workboats, the fishermen trolling slowly along, some with as many as a dozen lines out. Some sat still in the calm water, no doubt casting lines with lures or bait in the more traditional way. Everything seemed to fit a normal day on the water. And no sign of the General. Ben was a bit early, as he was for everything, so he cut the engine and drifted.

Soon, however, a typical bay workboat emerged from a tributary farther up the river and motored slowly toward him. Ben reached for the binoculars his dad kept on board and adjusted the focus to get a better view. He could only see a couple of men standing near the side of the vessel, and, of course, the captain as they drew nearer. Now he could make out General Briggs. He looked out of place in a light windbreaker, work trousers, and a straw hat. Ben could only grin.

As the boat came alongside, Sergeant Major Hammer reached for the rope Ben held out to him, and he lashed the two craft close together. "Good morning, Sergeant," the Sergeant Major said as he boarded the *Catalina*. "Nice boat. Oh. Permission to come aboard?"

Ben reached out to shake his hand and replied, "Of course, Sergeant Major." By now, the General was on board and, cigar in his left hand, shook Ben's hand with the other, and said, "Okay, let's get to it. We haven't much time. I need to know what you know. Anything that might be related to what happened to your folks, anything your friends might have told you, no matter how far-fetched it might sound. Especially your sheriff friend. He's been in on some of the investigations going on around here. Missing people and such. Right?"

General Briggs was as serious as Ben had seen him since they met and a little intimidating. Remembering that he had been told more than once to trust no one, Ben decided to share only a little about what had transpired in the past few days. He left out the sphere incident; Jim's investigation participation, limited as it was; and the visit by the two thugs Jim and Dave had encountered. He only shared that his friends had thought something quite weird was going on but couldn't explain it nor what to do about it.

Though the General eyed him in what Ben thought was a suspicious fashion, he seemed satisfied that what he learned was enough. He took a couple of thoughtful puffs from the cigar then looked Ben straight in the eye. "Okay. One more thing. You are being processed out of the Army. You'll not be returning to Germany."

Ben was stunned. He must be hearing wrong or something. He had done nothing wrong. As Ben opened his mouth to protest, the Sergeant Major put his hand on his shoulder. "Look, Sergeant, it has to be this way. For one thing, being an only child, you likely wouldn't have been able to enter the service, especially while we're in a war. It was your father who pulled some strings to make it happen. And now, well, you have inherited quite a substantial estate, with property, other assets, and so forth. Though not common, it's not unusual to discharge someone in your position. There's really nothing we can do. That's all there is to it, son. I think you could have had a promising career, and I, personally, hate to see this. You'll be okay, though. Just give it some time. You'll be getting a copy of your discharge and orders in a couple days. And arrangements have been made to have your personal items shipped from your unit and delivered to your home. We'll be in touch."

With that, they both boarded their boat, untied the rope holding the vessels together, and motored away.

Ben couldn't speak. What had just happened? How could it have happened. This just couldn't be.

His career, Allie. Oh god, Allie.

He started the *Catalina* and, at full throttle, headed home.

CHAPTER 8

The Boss had called in a small crew to clean up the mess
that was created when the sphere entered his office. The
smell would linger for a while, despite their best efforts to
clean, sanitize, and spray the room with everything they had on
hand. That made him furious at the thought of having to run
this operation in the stench that lingered. He told everyone to
leave, except for his newly appointed chief of operations.

"I'm tired of wasting my time playing with these clowns. Get
two of your best men, and send them to soldier boy's house.
Bring his aunt and cousin here. If they aren't there, find them.
Do whatever it takes, and let nothing get in the way. I hold
you responsible for the success of this job, you understand?
Do it now." The Boss was serious, as he always was. He had
no patience for screwups, as everyone knew. Guess that was
why the sharks hung around here every evening. "And find
that moron who left me here in this mess. When you do, feed
him to the fish, and report to me when you're done. Got it?
Now go, GO!"

The chief didn't even hang around long enough to acknowledge
the Boss's directions; he just left the room as quickly as he could.
Once outside the room, he rounded up whom he believed to
be two of his best men, disfigured as they were, briefed them
on their mission, and moved to the exit at the rear of the rusty

ship. There, they opened a nearly hidden door to find a small skiff waiting inside. From the wall nearest the door, the two accomplices each took a firearm from a rack where several arms of various types and sizes were stored. They climbed in the boat and headed out, first to the shallows of the bay; then, they steered into Fishing Creek. They could move along undetected till they got to the Dawson house, where they could creep ashore and take their quarry.

Though it took a while, they soon rounded the point and were within sight of the house. The chief directed the man at the helm to beach the boat among some tall reeds and cattails about fifty yards behind the property. Quietly they stepped out of the skiff and crept toward the backyard. As they went nearer the house, one of the men peered through the nearest window and saw three people inside, two women and a man. They all seemed preoccupied with conversation and didn't notice anything out of the ordinary.

Ben and Duke rounded the last corner and could finally see the house. He quickly shut the engine off and drifted toward the dock. Before he could even make contact with the bumpers that hung at the edge of the pier, Duke jumped from the boat and all but flew toward the house. Thinking the dog was just happy to be home, Ben didn't bother to call out to him. As he manually pulled the craft close to the nearest pylon, he readied the rope to secure it, first the front, then the rear, leaving enough slack to compensate for the changing tides. His mind on Allie, he had no idea what was taking place barely a hundred yards away.

*****

As the visitor drew back, the chief decided an all-out surprise home invasion would give them the best chance of success. They agreed the larger of the two men would neutralize the man inside while the other two would take the women. After agreeing on their method, they stepped back, firearm in hand, and ran toward the window. Crashing through the glass, each quickly came to their feet and moved toward their assigned targets before their victims could even turn their heads to see what was happening. The larger man threw Jim from his chair at the kitchen table, pinning him to the floor, holding the muzzle of the firearm to his neck. Jim could only lie motionless as he tried desperately to understand what was happening. Without warning, he felt the muzzle move away and, just as quickly, move toward his head as he blacked out. As Olivia screamed, the other man put his hand over her mouth, pulled her backward, and forced her to the floor. Unable to breathe, she soon passed out, but not before seeing her mother swing, at lightning speed, a frying pan of hot bacon and grease toward the other man. Though she made contact directly on his face, he threw a right fist at her head, and she fell limply to the floor as he cursed and wiped his face with his sleeve.

"Let's go. Quickly," he said as he mumbled some other unintelligible words under his breath.

As they moved with their quarry toward the window from which they had entered a moment ago, the chief caught a glimpse of something moving toward him at speed through that same opening. Duke, snarling with bared teeth, sunk most of those teeth into the neck of the would-be kidnapper. His grip loosened on Louise, and all three went to the floor. Seeing what had just happened, the larger man, with no load to carry, swung his firearm at the dog, knocking him across the kitchen floor with a yelp. Duke lay still where he landed, so the men left quickly the way they came.

With some effort, they were soon back in the skiff, the women bound and gagged, out of sight from anyone they might encounter, stuffed under a canvas wrap on the floor of the boat. The men smiled as they motored leisurely toward the bay. Except the chief, who was rubbing his face and mumbling obscenities to himself. Quietly he reached into his pocket and pushed a small button on the device he kept there. As a wisp of smoke in a breeze, the boat, with all its crew and passengers, vanished as if it had never existed.

*****

Ben approached the kitchen door, opened it, and stepped inside. Instead of seeing his aunt, his cousin, and Jim seated around the table, he saw an unnatural scene before him. Duke was stirring from his place on the floor, and beyond him lay Jim, slowly rubbing his head. Lifting Jim carefully, Ben asked, "What happened here? Where is Aunt Louise? And Olivia? Can you talk? Who did this?"

"Don't really know. Happened real fast. They came in through the window and moved so fast neither one of us had time to react. I'm guessing a planned kidnapping by professionals. They took the women out the window, I think." Jim was still a little lightheaded but seemed to be recovering from the blow he took.

Ben instantly jumped up, dove through the broken window, and ran into the backyard. Seeing no sign of anyone, he ran to the front of the house and scanned the long driveway. A lack of dust indicated the intruders either didn't leave by that route or left by boat. He ran quickly to the shoreline, scanned the creek, then ran as fast as he could toward the point. Hopefully, if they were still around, he could head them off there as they rounded the bend in the creek and headed toward the bay.

Winded but still on his feet, Ben looked around and saw no signs of any vessel, not even local crabbers or fishermen. He ran back to the house to see if Jim was okay and to check on Duke.

Entering through the kitchen door, he saw Jim sitting at the table, Duke pacing near his side. "Good boy, Duke. No wonder you took off from the boat so fast. You knew something was up, didn't you?" Duke licked Ben's outstretched hand, as if to let him know he understood.

"I think we need to call an emergency meeting, like, right now. Get Jack and Dave over here, and get to trying to find the girls. I'll call this in, and maybe we can get some help," Jim said as he got up and moved toward the phone.

"Call the guys, but not the police. Not yet, anyway," Ben said to Jim. 'I'm not sure who we can trust at this point, and I don't think we should involve anyone else until it's absolutely necessary. At least that's what my gut is telling me."

As Jim reached for the phone, it rang, almost startling them both. Jim lifted the handset and held it out to Ben.

Before Ben could say anything, a voice on the other end said, "Just listen, don't talk. If you want to see these women again, be at the location detailed for you in the note that has been left on your car. Be there at nine p.m. tonight, alone. You'll get instructions from there." And then a click as the caller hung up. Ben couldn't help but think that the voice on the other end sounded familiar. Nevertheless, this was a lot to process. The action he had planned to take after talking with the General earlier would have to wait. There was no time to waste. If he were a drinking guy, Ben figured this would be a good time to have a stiff one.

Ben motioned to Jim to follow him to the garage, with Duke accepting the invitation, as well.

Tucked under the right-side windshield wiper of the Impala, Ben found a folded piece of paper. Spreading it out on the hood of the car, he saw five words written in pencil: "Crocheron end of the world."

"What the heck does that mean?" asked Jim.

"You know where Crocheron is. If you go down there, as far as you can go, some folks refer to it as the 'end of the world.' You can't drive any further. Look to your left, Fishing Bay. To your right, the Chesapeake Bay. You'll go no further. At least not by car. And there's usually nobody around at night, anyway. Everybody's home, relaxing after a day on the water and with nothing to worry about except if the crabs will be in the pots when they check them in the morning." Jim seemed almost angry at the thought. Everyone else was going about their usually predictable lives, and here he was, tangled up with what appeared to be a madman, losing his parents, his aunt and his cousin taken in a violent intrusion, and not to mention, possibly losing the only girl he ever loved. Wow, that might be the first time that word ever crossed his mind since meeting Allie. Well, one thing at a time.

After Jim called Dave and Jack, they sat at the kitchen table to try to understand what was going on. They agreed that Dave might have a better theory about all this and an inventory of the facts that led up to it. Jim reiterated what little he knew of the mysterious disappearances that had occurred lately and how he figured they might be related to all this. He also threw out there the possibility that Ben's dad might have been on to something and that someone might think Ben knew something, as well.

"I don't know crap, except that we need to find out who is behind all this, get the women back safely, and me on a plane back to Germany," Ben said with the urgency clear in his voice.

It wasn't long before an old Chevy went rumbling up the driveway in a cloud of dust. The engine had barely stopped running when the two friends jumped out and practically ran to the door. Once inside the kitchen, they could hardly contain their anger as they saw the broken window, shards of glass on the floor, and the bump on Jim's head.

"I'm ready to kick some butt," Jack stated. He appeared to be prepared, judging by the Louisville Slugger he held in his hand.

"Well, we have to get a plan together first. We may only get one shot at this, so it has to be a good one. Dave, you've been filled in on everything. What's your take? And how do we move ahead?" Ben asked as all heads turned toward the smartest guy in the room. "And how'd you get here so fast?"

Dave, in his sometimes-thoughtful voice, simply answered, "New motor. Even more horsepower than the one I took out. There's still more left, and when we get this mess straightened out, I'm gonna find it.

"But to the point, I've done some research and a little pondering the past day or so. I'm certain this is all rooted in the Philadelphia Experiment, as I mentioned before."

Dave went on to lay out what he saw as evidence of his conclusion. The sphere, its ability to transport not only things but also people, to another location and, as he discovered, another time. To be specific, forward in time, about twenty-four hours, give or take a couple of minutes. He deduced this based on the clock on his wall and the glance at his watch when he ended up in that strange place. He showed them that his watch noted the day of the month in addition to the time of day. "It pays to notice details, you know," he said with a sly grin.

He went on to note that, as Ben's dad had worked in military intelligence, he could likely have known something about this sphere and who was messing around with it. Living in this region, so close to the unexplainable disappearances of a few people, had to be more than just a coincidence.

Either something on this property has someone on edge, or maybe it was just Ben's presence. Either way, whoever it was seemed to be getting impatient to go to such lengths as they had. It would appear that Ben, for whatever reason, was their target now. Or maybe all along.

Dave theorized that the note got on to the car in a similar fashion as the sphere appeared then disappeared, maybe by traveling in some way and carrying somebody with it.

Strange as Dave's theory was, it was all they had, and in a way, it kind of made sense. They all agreed, however, that if these people could make things vanish or move through time, they had best be careful.

"So I have a plan that I think will work. Maybe even offer some flexibility along the way. Always best to have a 'back door,' you know." Dave stated his plan simply and confidently. With a few hours to rest and gather the things they would need for the mission (Ben liked that word, *mission*), they ended their meeting to prepare for what would likely be a long night.

"Oh," Ben said, turning to Dave. "Where is that thing, the sphere, or ball, whatever it is?" With his typical trace of a grin, Dave answered, "They took it back, kind of just disappeared. No harm done."

The others knew from Dave's grin and short answer that he must have done something to make the return of the sphere a little more interesting than the owners might expect. The story of that "something" would have to wait for another time, though. Right now, there were more pressing matters to tend to. Jack and Dave left the kitchen and walked across the yard to the waiting Chevy.

"You ready, Jackson?" Dave asked his friend as they got into the car.

"Oh yeah. Let's go for the gusto, my friend. Take no prisoners." Jack seemed happy about the possibility of getting into a good scrap. Been a while, so it was due.

"What now?" asked Jim. "Don't really feel like just sitting here doing nothing." Ben pondered that question for a bit. Jim was right; they couldn't just do nothing.

"How about you go see what you can dig up on the disappearance investigations—who they are, where they were, or were supposed to be. I think that the more we know, the better off we'll be. Maybe some of that information could help in some way."

"Okay. What about you? I know you're not going to sit around and wait to walk into a hornet's nest or God knows what." Jim was genuinely concerned about Ben and was afraid his friend might jump the gun and really get into trouble, trouble he couldn't get out of.

"Well, I'm going to start by making a phone call. I need to call my unit in Germany. That might put me at ease and let me focus on what might be coming my way here." He tried to sound calm and confident, but inside, his gut was churning in time to his rapid heartbeat. *How could things get so bad so fast? And how was it all going to end? Guess we would know by morning.*

CHAPTER 9

B en was growing impatient as the telephone at the other end continued to ring. There was always someone there to answer calls, even after duty hours. It was nearing the end of the workday at his unit in Germany, but even if everyone had left early, the charge of quarters was at his desk to take calls. And if he was called away, his assistant, or runner, as he was called, would man the phone.

After hanging up, Ben waited a few minutes and tried again. Just as before, no one picked up. He then called the number for the battalion headquarters. Surely there would be someone there to take calls. After only a couple of seconds, someone did pick up. "First Thirty-Third Battalion Headquarters, Specialist Franklin."

"This is Sergeant Dawson, Headquarters Battery," Ben said into the phone. "I tried the unit, and no one answered, and I need to get a message to someone. I'm in the States, and it looks like I won't be coming back. Can you help me?"

"Oh," said the Specialist, "everybody's gone. We had an alert, something about a terrorist attack on a General up north, so everybody got alerted and called out to a staging area. I can't tell you any more than that. Operational security, you know."

"Can you tell me if it was just us or how widespread is it?" Ben was getting frustrated now. "How about our support unit?"

"Can't say any more. I can try to get a message out for you, though. Don't know when it'll get delivered, 'cause I don't know exactly what's going on or for how long," the young soldier stated.

"Guess that'll have to do. I need to get this message to Specialist Allie Morgan, 156th Maintenance Company. She works with the Contact Team in our motor pool. She has to call me at this number as soon as possible." Ben gave him his number and had him repeat it to ensure he had it correctly noted.

"Okay, Sarge, I'll do my best. Like I said, I just don't know when it'll happen." Franklin didn't sound confident it would happen anytime soon.

"Well, do your best. Please, it's important," said Ben. "Thanks."

That sure turned to crap pretty quick, thought Ben. They had alerts all the time, but it was always for training or standard local deployments. This must be a pretty big deal to send everyone out. But precautions had to be taken, especially in Western Europe, where terrorist activity would pop up when you least expected it. Nothing to do now but try to get some rest. A long night lay ahead, and the gang had best be on their toes.

Getting any rest was going to be difficult enough, but up the driveway came that red Corvette. That could only mean Sarah. This was going to be a short visit, for sure.

"Duke, you ready to help get rid of somebody?"

Duke barked in the affirmative and stood beside Ben, ready to do anything he was asked. After all, Duke wasn't too crazy about this particular human, either.

*****

In a dimly lit room, devoid of any furnishings, Louise and Olivia sat on a wool blanket spread out across the floor. Still a bit confused and disoriented from their recent ordeal, they leaned against the wall, trying to make sense of it. Neither of them had any sense of where they might be, and without any windows to the outside for reference, neither did they know if it was day or night.

Louise reached out and gently stroked Olivia's cheek. "You okay, baby?"

"Yeah, I think so. How about you?" she replied. She was clearly weak and moved her arms about carefully to reassure herself they were still attached.

"Yes, I'm okay. Just a little sore. We have to try to figure out where we are and why this happened," she stated calmly. Indeed, this was an utter surprise to them both, as well as a bit scary. They had no idea what might happen to them and who might go to such lengths to take them captive. And where was Jim? Did they leave him at the house? Or worse?

As they lay there quietly, they could hear people scurrying about beyond the only door to the room. Now and then they could hear someone come close, but they kept moving with seemingly little interest in the room where the pair was being held.

"No matter what, we try to stay together." Louise was serious and looked directly into Olivia's eyes as she made that statement.

"Yes," replied Olivia. "Yes, we will."

"Things might get a little confusing and start moving very quickly later on," Louise continued, "but I want you to listen to me and stay close. There may not be time to ask questions.

We can sort things out later. I promise." She held Olivia close as she talked, trying to reassure her that everything would be alright. If only she could fully believe it herself.

Soon they were both getting drowsy as fatigue and stress overtook them. Holding each other, they drifted off into a light, fitful sleep.

*****

Jack and Dave rounded the corner on the little-used long dirt road that snaked through the marshes behind Dave's house. Ahead, almost hidden by the tall sea grasses that grew in abundance in this part of the county, lay the summer cottage his dad had built many years ago. It was a simple small structure, little more than a place to spend some quiet time while looking out over the bay.

Dave fondly remembered spending many hours there, studying, solving complicated mathematical formulas, and pondering the physics of all that is. This place offered the solitude to study and work undisturbed, except when his mother brought him lunch or snacks. Dave still kept a few snacks and "emergency food" here, secure in a sealed locker, for those infrequent visits. Water was made available with a roof-mounted cistern that caught rainwater that was gravity-fed to a small sink in the kitchen area. There were no modern indoor toilet facilities, as the little house wasn't intended for long-term stays.

The two men who had earlier tried, though half-heartedly, to cause them harm should still be holed up safely inside. Though the occupants promised to do no harm and, in fact, to help them if they could, they were prepared should they encounter a change of heart by the two men inside. Especially Jack, who now carried his Louisville Slugger everywhere he went.

Jack was the first to see movement at one of the front windows as the curtain inside was pulled back slightly. It appeared these two guys were on alert and stayed on the lookout for anyone approaching. Upon seeing who was walking up the road, someone opened the front door slowly, and one of the men stood there to greet them.

"It's just us, we've come to talk," Dave said, holding up one hand to show he had no weapon. The man at the door looked at Jack with apprehension. "What about him?"

"He's okay, he just likes to be prepared," Dave said with a grin.

The man stepped back, and Jack and Dave entered the first of only two rooms. This was the living area, with a primitive small kitchen on the left side. Ahead was a large window through which you could enjoy an uninterrupted view of the bay beyond.

The second man sat in a rocking chair near the rear window and watched closely as Jack and Dave made their way to a couple of wooden chairs, placed against the front wall.

"My name is Wilber Tawes, that's Merrit Thomas. You may have heard of us," the first, taller man said. He spoke with a discernible sadness in his voice. That sadness became obvious after Jack and Dave heard their names.

Wilber Tawes disappeared one day a couple of months ago while working his crab pots out near the bay. When he failed to return home, his wife notified the Coast Guard and then the police. After they searched his last known location for several days, Wilber was presumed lost, perhaps because of a failure of his equipment or maybe his boat struck an object just beneath the water's surface, resulting in his boat sinking before he could send a distress call. An experienced boat captain, he had worked these waters for decades, following in his father's footsteps. Though his area of choice was near Bloodsworth Island, where nautical charts alerted sailors of the dangers there and clearly identified the restricted, forbidden areas surrounding the island, he, like other watermen, stayed well clear of the area.

Adding to the mystery of his disappearance was the fact that no debris of any kind was ever found. No wood fragments, oil slick, or other flotsam. The authorities had little choice but to declare him lost at sea and end their investigation, much to the disappointment and sadness of his family.

Not long after Wilber's disappearance, Merrit vanished under much the same circumstances just a couple of weeks later. During a typical day on the water, he, too, failed to return home. Just as in Wilber's case, no debris was ever found, again after many days of searching. He was also declared lost at sea, and his case closed, as well. Coincidental? Maybe not.

"Yes, we heard about both of you. But you're here, alive. Why not go home, notify the police or someone?" Dave asked, a little baffled.

"Well," Merrit began. "Our stories are the same. One minute we're goin' about our work, just like every other day, then everything got a little fuzzy. Next thing we knew, though, things seemed to clear up some. There was a strangeness to it. No other boats around, no noise, not even the gulls. Everything seemed to have gone away except us. Then I realized my arm was stuck into the boat. I mean right into the wood. The pain was nothing like I ever felt before, and I passed out. Next thing I knew, I was waking up in what looked like a hospital room, 'cept it wasn't no hospital. And I had this metal arm. Don't know how it come about, but it did."

Wilber then shared his story, as strange as Merrit's.

"Same with me. Pulling pots one minute, then that fuzzy feelin'. Then that silence. The pain came on then, and I saw my leg stuck into the boat, and my head hurt like never before. Passed out, woke up in a room just like Merrit. 'Cept I had this metal leg and a hunk of metal in my head."

Merrit spoke up with more revelations. "Couple days later, this guy came into the room where me and Wilber were and told us we were going to work for him. And if we didn't, they'd do to our families just what they did to us, including our kids. He was mean as a snake, I could tell. And we knew he meant business 'cause he told us where we lived, our wives' names, names of our kids, everything. Hard as it was, we decided to agree until we could figure out something. He said he'd do to us what he did to some teenagers, send them off somewhere so's they'd never get back.

"Yeah, so we've just been doing work around his laboratory since then. Till they sent us after you. Didn't tell us why, just said get rid of you both, any way we could. But it ain't in us to kill nobody." Wilber spoke with sincerity, again showing a sadness that lived deep inside him.

"There's a couple more like us there, too, and they feel the same way we do," Merrit added. "They're just waiting like we are for some way to get out of this mess without doin' our families in. So if you guys got a plan, we'd like to hear it. There's about six of us that will help you." The desperation in his voice came across loud and clear. Wilber nodded, with eyes begging for help.

*****

Ben opened the kitchen door as Sarah was walking toward the house. Duke bounded out to greet her, sniffed her outstretched hand, then quickly returned to sit beside his human.

"Well, hello," she said cheerfully. "Thought I'd stop by to see how you're doing." Not content to remain outside, she slowly brushed a little too closely by Ben and turned toward him as she stood in the kitchen. Duke moved to her side and stood, gazing at her. She glanced quickly down at him and met his icy stare. She appeared a bit uneasy, which was just fine with Ben.

"I'm doing okay. Just taking care of some family business, stuff that has to be done." He didn't want to appear worried or concerned about anything, at least no more than one might expect, given the circumstances.

"Anything I can do to help? After all, I do work in a law office. Maybe I can help translate some of the papers you have to go through." She sounded far too eager to get into Ben's business. She had an uncanny way of sniffing out money or at least the prospect of getting a piece of someone else's. Not going to happen today.

"No, thanks. I don't think it'll be too difficult. Mr. Sterling has it all sorted out and easy to get through." Ben hoped that would be enough to get her off the subject.

"Well," she began, "I just want to make sure you're okay. You've been through a lot lately, and I know it can take a toll. I thought I could look at things from an outside viewpoint, you know, with a bit more clarity. Kind of help you sort stuff out."

"I can see things clear enough. I just need a little time to myself to focus on what's important and take things one step at a time." While true, he figured she might understand, as well as she could, and take the hint that he didn't need her around.

"Well," she said as she gave him a short kiss on the cheek, "I'm always a call away. Who knows, maybe this summer we can spend some time together, you know, catch up on the past few years since high school. See you later, Ben."

With that, she turned and let herself out. Ben watched her get into her car, sensing something was all wrong with their conversation, but he couldn't put his finger on it. There was enough to do and worry about right now, though, so maybe it would come to him later.

He looked at the clock and realized it would only be a few hours before he had to get down to Crocheron to see what surprises awaited. Hopefully, Jack and Dave could come up with a plan that would keep everything from going too crazy and maybe even get to the bottom of all this.

Fighting the urge to pick up the phone and call his unit again, he went into the living room and sat in the nearest recliner. As Ben pulled the lever on the side of the chair to fully recline, Duke moved next to him and lay on the floor, letting out a deep sigh. He, too, could feel the stress in the air and sensed that there was much more to come.

Though his mind was reeling, Ben closed his eyes, knowing that he would need all the rest and strength he could muster for the hours ahead. It wasn't long before he fell into a shallow, restless sleep, thoughts of Allie dominating his thoughts.

*****

Holding her hand, Ben and Allie walked along the quiet streets of a small German town in a place called Fränkische Schweiz, or Little Switzerland, located near the Bavarian Alps. The town lay in a peaceful long valley, following a small river that ran from one end to the other. The entire valley meandered for over twenty-five miles, dotted with typical old Bavarian-styled villages, framed on the east and west by forested hills and green meadows occupied by well-cared-for cattle and sheep. Everywhere you looked, it seemed as if you were looking at a postcard.

As they rounded a corner, a German woman, sweeping the cobblestones in front of her open door, looked at them and smiled. "Ihr seht gut aus Zusammen," she said to them, halting her chore for a moment to watch them pass. "Danke," Ben answered, returning her smile as he looked at Allie. Giving him a puzzled look, she asked, "What did she say?" Smiling and pulling her close, Ben replied, "She said we looked good together." Looking into her eyes as she smiled at him, he kissed her gently. "She's right, you know. We do look good together."

*****

Ben woke to the sound of the phone ringing in the kitchen. He quickly rose, and still half asleep, he grabbed the receiver and answered, "Hello. This is Ben." It was Dave on the other end. "Okay, buddy, we've got a plan together. Don't worry, you won't be alone tonight, but you likely won't see us. We've enlisted some help, and we're going to try to end this nonsense once and for all." He spoke firmly and confidently, not giving Ben a chance to even reply or ask any questions. "Make sure you're rested, and go where you have been told. You'll see when it's over, and you may be surprised at who is on our side. See you later, my friend. We have preparations to make." With that, Dave hung up.

Well, that's good to know, Ben thought. He had no idea what they had come up with, but Dave was a smart guy, and he had surely thought things out carefully.

Looking at the clock, Ben realized it was time to go. It was a long drive from here, and he didn't want to be late for this date with destiny.

"Well, Duke," he said to his companion. The dog was sitting patiently on the floor beside him and whined softly. He sensed something sinister awaited his master, and it made the hair stand up along his back. "I'll be back."

After making sure Duke had sufficient food and water accessible and enough to last a couple of days, Ben went to the garage. He first removed a service revolver from the hidden safe, loaded it, and tucked it under his belt behind his back, where he hoped it wouldn't be noticeable. Then, taking the keys for the pickup from the hook on the wall, he pushed the button on the garage-door opener, climbed into the cab, and started the engine.

After a couple of seconds, he placed the transmission in gear and backed out, closing the door behind him.

As he turned to go down the long lane, he looked back at the house and wondered if he would ever see it again.

The drive to Crocheron took nearly an hour, maybe because he had intentionally driven slower than usual to prolong his freedom and delay what might lie ahead. The darkness, fighting successfully against the crescent moon, which hung low on the horizon, enveloped him despite the headlights of the truck guiding the way. His stomach in knots, Ben truly felt he was going to the end of the world, a dark, foreboding place full of unspeakable monsters and men who held the power of life and death in their hands. Being a mere mortal, Ben realized that no matter what plan the guys had come up with, they would be no match for what they had already experienced, let alone the terror that waited beyond the waters of Fishing Bay.

Ben soon stopped the truck at the bulkhead that signaled the end of his journey. Beyond lay the bay, made all the more eerie by just enough light to make out dead trees, abandoned pylons, and the black silhouette of the distant shoreline. He shut the truck off, dousing the lights as he got out and walked to the water's edge.

The night was quiet, with the only sound being the gentle lapping of the small waves against the bulkhead, trying desperately to reach up and grab Ben's feet to pull him to his demise.

A shiver went up Ben's spine, causing him to inhale deeply. As Ben exhaled, a fuzzy feeling came over him, and as if he had never existed, he vanished.

From the tall sea grass near the bulkhead where Ben had been standing only a second ago came a rustling sound. Four figures slowly stood, gazing in wonderment at the spot that now held no one.

To one side stood the two watermen who had gone along to assist in their mission. To the other stood Dave and Jack, the latter holding tight to his Louisville Slugger.

Dave spoke softly, to no one in particular. "Sure didn't expect that."

CHAPTER 10

As the men stood within the sea grass, staring in disbelief at what had just happened to their friend, the lights came on in the nearby crab house. Though it had appeared abandoned, in need of paint and extensive repairs, there was obviously electricity still running to it. A rickety door creaked open, and four men dressed in what looked like military tactical gear stepped outside into the gloom, separating evenly to each side, moving cautiously toward the surprised observers. Behind them, a slightly taller figure walked casually toward them, now flanked by the four black-clad figures. At the door stood another figure, remaining silhouetted against the building's interior lighting.

As they grew closer, it became clear they each carried a weapon of some sort. Other pieces of equipment were secured to small harnesses they wore, maybe radios, ammunition, or some type of support gear.

Though the taller figure was dressed in a similar fashion, there were no outward signs of weapons of any kind, at least as far as could be seen. It was a woman. She strode with the confidence of a professional in whatever field she was in, a leader, for sure. Dave wondered if she might be an assassin or something close. He wondered if everyone else was suffering from the same rapid heartbeat and dry mouth he was dealing with at that moment.

Dave and the two watermen were of average height. Jack, however, stood a good six inches taller than his friends. This mysterious woman matched his height, making her an even more imposing sight on this strange night.

She stopped within a few feet of the silent onlookers, eyeing each one up, maybe to see which one deserved to feel the blade of her dagger or receive the first round from her hidden pistol. When she got to Jack, the only one not requiring a downward gaze, she paused for a moment, the trace of a smile growing across her lips. Looking down at his Louisville Slugger, she said softly, "Now, now, cowboy. Why don't you just drop that before you hurt yourself." Almost instantly, the bat fell to the ground with a thud.

Having inspected the group and finding herself satisfied, she took a couple of steps backward. "My name is Flynn, Agent Pepsy Flynn. Let's go inside, and I'll brief you boys, at least as much as I can," she said as she motioned toward the small building.

Once they were inside the building, the lighting was better, and the details of each of the mysterious assembly of soldiers became easily discernible. Four of the men were indeed soldiers or law enforcement. They were muscular and stern-faced and showed no signs of emotion whatsoever. Whatever they were, they meant business. The man that had remained at the door was a middle-aged man, distinguished looking, but an expression of fear showed all over his chubby face.

The woman was a different story. Relatively tall, attractive, with an air of confidence about her, she had to be the leader of this band of commandos. She stood erect, arms crossed across her chest, and visually assessed Dave and his friends. Again, she gazed at Jack for just a couple of seconds longer than she had the others, a slight smile forming on her lips.

As they gathered inside the shack, two of the other men remained outside. Flynn spoke first, looking at Dave, Jack, Merrit, and Wilber. "First, I can tell you all that you have been under surveillance for some time, including Jim and Ben. As a matter of fact, we have been watching Ben since just before he left Germany. And not only to monitor your whereabouts but for your safety. We've also been closely watching the man responsible for all you're going through. We've been able to secure some of the victims of his experiments, too. We have four teenagers in safekeeping that would have otherwise been dead by now. I'm afraid there have been a few others we were unable to get to. They'll never be seen again. This may be our last opportunity to end this before there are more casualties. He has become a national-security risk, worse than anything we've faced before."

Dave spoke up. "Then why have you let him keep doing all this weird stuff? And he took Ben, didn't he?"

"Because we need to nail his coconspirators, as well as him. We believe that now that he has Ben, he'll want to show him off to them. It's an ego thing." She punctuated that phrase with a smile aimed directly at Jack. He couldn't help but return a smile, accompanied by a rarely seen blush.

Flynn continued, "We've had to be very careful with this operation. If he went underground with it, we might never be able to get our hands on the whole crew again. We think he knows we're watching him and he's getting desperate."

As the group exchanged glances, she continued.

"This guy has ties to the area, as well as close allies within the government. We suspect someone at the Pentagon, even the Department of Defense, is involved. That's how he got his ship. It sits out near the bay, in a restricted area, so no one can get near it. It was once used by the Navy for target practice, but the interior has been refurbished and turned into the ideal place for him to carry out his dirty work. But he seems to have carried out his plans as far as he can go with what he has. And he has some pretty sophisticated equipment, most of it stolen technology from our own government, as well as some other advanced countries. You'd be surprised at just what he has in there.

"That's why he needs Ben. He's missing a piece of the puzzle. He's convinced Ben's father gave something to his son that will be key to achieving his ultimate goal. Right now, he can move anyone or anything forward in time, though by only about twenty-four hours. Into tomorrow, if you will. His goal is to move backward in time. That would be disastrous in his hands."

"The Philadelphia Experiment," Dave interjected.

Agent Flynn smiled at him. "Congratulations, my friend. That's exactly what started all this. Though it was shelved as an unsuccessful attempt to render Navy vessels invisible, he has somehow gained access to the technology, albeit on a smaller scale. Now he seems fixated on the time travel and transport aspect of it. With some success, I might add.

"So you can see the potential security issues here. If he could move himself or anyone he can trust forward and backward in time, he can direct the path of history how he sees fit. Add to that the transport advantage, it becomes even more troublesome, to say the least. He'll no doubt weaponize it for his benefit. Money, power, influence. All things that people like him can only dream of. He could, literally, change the world into one in which he can rule without opposition. And given the chance, he will, and it won't be pretty. And for those who oppose him, he can send them into that place that's always tomorrow."

Dave couldn't help but notice that, as she spoke, her eyes were almost always on Jack. His friend sat still and quiet, gazing back at her like a lovestruck schoolboy. Dave elbowed him, just to see if he could break the spell. Nope, he didn't even notice, so he figured he'd join the discussion.

"What's the plan then? And how do we extract everyone safely? We've got friends in there, you know."

The chubby man, who had remained silent until now, spoke up. "I'm Ian, one of the scientists working on the project. I've been keeping Agent Flynn's division up to speed on what happens out in the ship. I was recruited by the Boss, as he is called, because of my work with the government. Agent Flynn thought it would be a good idea to have someone on the inside. Anyway, it's easy to see the military possibilities of this work. Trouble is, we've only been able to squeeze twenty-four hours out of it, and that's with all the power we feel we can feed it. We're limited as far as our equipment too. Only get so much technology into that old ship and still keep it under wraps. As a result, the range and strength of each orb are limited."

"Think of it as a bubble," Dave stated. "The more power, the bigger the bubble. So with what power is available now, an area about twenty or thirty feet in diameter can be moved, either forward in time or to another location. The distance is also dictated by the power supply. How far can it reach currently, Ian?"

Ian nodded in approval of Dave's grasp of the theories in play here. "Right now, about twenty-five or thirty miles from the power source," Ian said, stroking his chin. "Makes a pretty big circle. But since we've been reducing power, that circle is getting smaller, and he knows it. Just maybe not why. That's why he had to get Ben to come closer before he could grab him. And as Flynn stated earlier, we can't let him figure out how to go back in time."

Once again, Dave joined in the discussion. "Temporal paradox. Should effect precede its cause, temporal paradox is created, which is a violation of causality."

"Explain that in English, brainiac," Jack said.

Dave continued, "You can't change something that has already happened. So here we sit, for example. If I went back in time and tied you to a pole so you couldn't get here, that would create the temporal paradox. 'Cause you're here, now. See the problem?"

Ian seemed impressed with Dave's familiarity with these theories. "You have quite an understanding of what's going on here, my friend. We could solve a lot of problems together. Yes, quite an understanding."

Flynn wrapped up the meeting. "We're going to get this over with tonight. We'll get Ben and the others out of there and contain the ones we need to. So you guys," she said while looking at Jack and Dave, "go home and wait there. We can handle it. We have everything in place, and we're ready to move." She looked directly at Jack as she stood.

"I'll see you later, cowboy. It shouldn't take long. There are only five or six orbs that we know of, and we have two of them, so we can travel pretty quick. I'll send two agents with you, two will go with me, along with you, too, Ian. We have a team of special operations guys ready to move and a sub nearby in the bay, with another team at the ready. Time is running out, so let's move."

Jack liked the way she took control of everything. There was a lot more about this woman he wanted to know, but it would have to wait. One thing was for sure: she was going to get her way—and it looked like she was used to that.

She looked at her watch. It didn't look like any you could find at the local department store or even at a fine jeweler. Small though it was, there were tiny buttons around the perimeter and a simple yet finely constructed dial. After informing them they had only seven minutes, she directed two agents to take Jack and Dave to the side.

"See you later, cowboy. Don't forget your Slugger."

Jack, Dave, the two watermen, and the two agents moved to the edge of the gravel parking area. Jack turned to meet Flynn's gaze as she blew him a kiss. Still looking at him, she said, "Two minutes." She then turned to stand next to Ian and the other two agents.

Though the agents that stood with Jack and Dave were calm, Dave was as excited as a child waiting in line for his first ride on the newest, most terrifying ride at the carnival. He could barely contain his anticipation. He didn't know what to expect, but he knew it would be like nothing he had ever experienced. And it would probably be fun.

As a fuzzy feeling overtook the four, Jack looked once more at the mysterious Agent Flynn, just in time to catch her smile as darkness set in; then, just like that, they were standing in Ben's front yard.

*****

Ben found himself in a dark place. No top or bottom, just a strange, disoriented feeling; stifling; and a feeling that each breath he took would use up what little air surrounded him. Just as he thought he could bear no more, he found himself in a dimly lit office of some sort. He could make out a couch, a couple of plush chairs, and a carpet beneath his feet. The faint odor of what he recognized as similar to low tide filled his nostrils, certainly out of place in the environment he found himself in.

In front of him stood a large desk, behind which sat a shadowy figure, his back toward him. The figure moved slightly, turned around in the swivel chair, and faced him. Leaning forward over the desk and into the faint light, Ben was able to make out his features. He was stunned to see that he was face-to-face with Mr. Sterling. Confused and speechless, he could only stand there in disbelief as the figure stood and leaned further toward him.

"Well, good to see you, Master Ben," Mr. Sterling said sarcastically. "Glad you could join us."

Out of the shadows stepped General Briggs, the Sergeant Major, Sarah, and two other men Ben didn't recollect seeing before. As they were dressed in white lab coats, he could only surmise they were medical personnel, doctors, maybe.

But what were they doing here? Ben asked himself. If this was part of some sinister operation, they shared at least one thing in common: a desire to get something from him. Now it seemed to be coming together. The General probing for information and wanting to know what Ben knew, where he went, and who he might be with. And Sarah, being her nosy self, wanting the same information, always showing up at the house and other places. And the comment about having "all summer" to hang out together. She must have known he wouldn't be going back to Germany before he even had a chance to tell her.

Mr. Sterling got right to the point. "I think you have something I want, and I don't have time to play, so where is it?"

"I have no idea what you're talking about. And it was you, wasn't it? My parents, my discharge from the Army to keep me here." Ben was growing angry as things started to make some sense. "I have nothing you want, and I'm not so sure I'd give it to you even if I did."

Mr. Sterling seemed to be getting angry as well. "Maybe we can arrange a trade. What you have for what I have. You would like to see the girls again, wouldn't you?"

General Briggs interjected. "Your father gave you something. He made sure that not all information was kept in the same place. He liked to spread things around. Security concerns, you know? So think, boy. You may not know exactly what it is, but you have to know it's important. Just as important as your aunt and cousin, don't you think?"

Ben struggled to think of something, anything he might have seen or received from his father. There was the file he found in the garage safe, but though he didn't understand much of what he saw in the folder, it didn't seem that important. Or maybe it was. That had to be it.

Before he could speak, Mr. Sterling said, "Enough of this. You go think a bit, and we'll give you one more chance to do the right thing."

Almost instantly, Ben found himself in that gray place again, no top or bottom, floating in air that grew thinner by the minute.

*****

Flynn held up her left hand as she looked at the chronograph on her right. "Okay, go time," she said. Had anyone been watching, they would have seen the small group vanish in front of them. No bang, whoosh, or smoke. Just gone, quietly and completely.

Back at Ben's house, Duke, who was standing at the front window with his paws on the sill, growled softly as a small assembly of humans suddenly appeared in the front yard.

"I've really gotta get me one of these," Dave said to no one in particular.

CHAPTER 11

O nce again, Ben found himself in the office he had left only moments before. This time, the lights had been turned up, allowing him to see his surroundings more clearly. This time, however, they were joined by Aunt Louise and Olivia. The doctors, or whatever they were, stood on either side of the women. Ben began to speak, but Aunt Louise nodded to him, an assurance that they were okay, at least for the moment.

Mr. Sterling spoke first. "I thought we'd have a little family reunion. Where we go from here is up to you, Master Ben. Home or to a place where it's always tomorrow. You know the place. You've been there a couple times. Not a particularly pleasant place, but then I like to know where everyone is. Your choice."

Ben grappled with the thoughts that were spinning around in his mind, as if every word he knew were in a blender. This was surreal, downright unbelievable. It was enough that he was a target for a band of madmen, but to bring Aunt Louise and Olivia into it was just too much to comprehend. This nightmare was his and his alone. They had nothing to do with any of it, and the thought of it brought his anger to a point where it overwhelmed any rational thought or answer that might come to bear.

His throat dry, his mind reeling, he began to try to form something coherent, something reasonably intelligible that he could speak that might satisfy this already-unreasonable collection of single-minded individuals. Maybe he could bluff them, at least long enough to come up with some kind of plan to get the women out of here. But as insane as they might be, they were certainly intelligent and would likely see through anything he might come up with. That could anger them enough to do something even worse to the women and to himself, for sure.

Words began forming in his throat even as he knew he wouldn't even know what those words would be until they were spoken. As he opened his mouth, praying for divine intervention, the lights went out, sending them all into a blackness that was even darker than tomorrow and just as menacing.

*****

Now in position, standing in the narrow hall just outside the office door, Agent Flynn softly said, "Three, two," and as she said "one," one of her men placed a device against the coded lock beside the door. Instantly, a soft click could be heard, and the second agent shouldered the door open as the lights went out. In a carefully planned execution, Flynn placed a powerful magnetic strobe light against the inside wall. The result was as they had hoped. The occupants, caught completely off guard by the unexpected intrusion, stood frozen and disoriented.

Just as quickly, as if it had been carefully rehearsed, the two agents rushed the doctors, pinning them against the wall. In a move that astonished Ben, Aunt Louise stepped in front of Sarah, spun like a top, and landed a swift, powerful kick to the unsuspecting girl's head. She went down like a felled tree in a heap of lipstick, makeup, and designer clothes.

In the same instant, the Sergeant major put General Briggs in a chokehold that rendered him unconscious, sending him to the deck in unison with Sarah and just as incapacitated. The move of the day, however, had to go to Agent Flynn. As all the others were being dealt with, Flynn sailed across the office as if on wings, headed straight to a landing on Mr. Sterling. Just as she was about to reach him with her outstretched hands, he vanished. With nothing to stop or slow her momentum, she skidded across the desktop, sending the phone and lamp skittering to the wall ahead of her. She made contact with that same wall a split second later and slid helplessly to the carpeted floor.

Ian, who had been standing safely by the door, reached in, turning off the strobe light as the office lights flickered on. A smile appeared on his face as if he alone had orchestrated the previous event, and basked in its success. Lot of help he was, Ben thought.

Now that the melee was over and the lights were on, Ben could see the results of the short struggle. Though it had lasted for less than thirty seconds, the scene revealed who the victors were. Sarah lay on the floor in a heap, moaning, probably more worried about her makeup than any wounds she may have endured. The General remained where he fell, after being on the receiving end of an effective move on the part of the Sergeant Major. As their eyes met, the Sergeant Major just winked and smiled. Ben sure hoped these guys were on his side. If not, real trouble lay ahead.

His survey of the damage done by this small but obviously well-trained team was interrupted by moaning sounds coming from behind the desk. Flynn stood and assessed her condition, counting her limbs and muttering to herself. She stepped cautiously from her landing spot and gave a quick glance around the room.

"Well done, people," she said, and moved to stand in front of Ben. "I'm Agent Flynn. Pepsy Flynn. Don't ask me who we work for. If I told you, I'd have to shoot you. I know who you are, so we can dispense with any further introductions."

Somehow Ben figured she might indeed shoot him. After what he had just witnessed, anything was possible.

Flynn continued, directing her attention to the other agents and anyone left standing. "Let's get this mess cleaned up. Secure the actors and the vessel. Contact the other teams, and let them know they can move in. They know what to do." She turned her attention to Ben once again. "Thought for sure we had him, but in this business, you just never know until you know." Motioning toward the ladies and Ian, she continued, "Okay, stand close and hang on." She nodded her head to one of her agents, and the five of them were instantly standing in Ben's front yard.

She turned to Ben and simply stated, "We have the updated version. Works quicker than his. Someplace we can collect ourselves and discuss our next moves?" A dazed Ben answered, "Sure, this way." and they walked toward the house.

Flynn stayed behind long enough to speak to her agents, gesturing toward different parts of the property. As they departed to their assigned areas, she joined the parade to the house.

As Ben opened the kitchen door, Duke bounded out, whining as he circled the group. When he had completed the second lap around them, he stopped and jumped upward, putting his massive front feet on his master's shoulders. Still whining, in a joyful way, he licked Ben's face as though he had not seen him in decades. "It's okay, boy." Ben assured him as the dog returned to his four-feet-on-the-ground position.

He quickly sniffed at each of them, stopping briefly at Ian, at which time he stood completely still and stared up at the man. Having gained any information he needed, he accompanied them all to the kitchen.

Jack and Dave were standing at the kitchen table and greeted them as they entered. Though they were eager to learn about what had happened the last hours, they knew they could catch up later. Jack smiled at Agent Flynn as she moved around the table toward him. "Miss me, cowboy?" she said as she reached out and tapped his nose with her forefinger.

All Jack could do was nod with a red face. The guys would have to talk to him later about his reaction to Flynn, reactions they had never seen from him since they had known him. Curious, indeed.

As some sat at the table and others stood, Flynn, standing at one end of the table, looked around the room and began. "I can fill you all in on a little bit now, only what you need to know since you're all involved in this to some extent."

She continued now that she had everyone's attention. "As some of you have figured out, this is all related to the Philadelphia Experiment that was conducted back in the forties. As we mentioned before, somehow, Sterling and his cohorts got hold of it. We don't know how deep this goes into the government, but we do know he heads up an ongoing plan to weaponize the technology and use it for nefarious purposes.

"We've been monitoring him and his team for quite a while but felt it was time to move in." She turned to Ben and said, "We're sorry we were unable to save your parents. We didn't think he would go to that length to try to move his operation forward. After that, we increased or manpower and with Ian's help, we were able to secure two orbs and get them working for our team.

"You have also pretty much figured out the theory behind the technology and how the operation relates to the available power. That's why we've gained control of the power that goes to his vessel and into his laboratories.

"He made a lot of mistakes once he decided to focus more on the 'travel' part of the time-travel abilities." She looked around the table and saw she had everyone mesmerized by her revelations.

"The earth travels at over sixty-six thousand miles per hour around the sun. In addition, it spins at over one thousand miles per hour on its axis."

Dave, proud of himself to be able to contribute to this conversation, said, "Because of that movement, when you go forward in time, you don't come back to the same place or time. Kind of like standing on a moving platform. You jump straight up, the platform continues moving, you come back down, but not where you jumped from." He looked seriously at Flynn. "That explains the injuries these men sustained. They went forward, and when they came back, the earth had moved, the ship with it. They ended up either partially or completely mixed in with the superstructure."

Everyone was silent, some looking sorrowfully at Wilber and Merrit. They were the lucky ones, though. Others had been completely consumed by whatever they had come back to.

Flynn added, "And remember, tomorrow is not here yet, so if you end up there, it's kind of like limbo, waiting for the rest of us but moving forward proportionately. With the orbs and enough calculation, you could find yourself in a time-warped field, a self-contained field in which time rates within it can be accelerated or decelerated relative to the time outside the field. Sterling was close to that we think, and the ramifications could be disastrous."

Dave asked, "So is it kind of 'tuned in' to existing time?"

Flynn answered simply, "Sterling wants to move backward in time, creating the temporal paradox I mentioned earlier."

Except Dave and Ian, everyone seemed stunned and confused at these explanations. Ian was more matter-of-fact about it, while Dave grew more excited with each new bit of information that was shared. It was clear he had found something he could have a great deal of fun with if he had access to the equipment and personnel.

"Where do you think Sterling went?" Ben asked.

Ian answered, "Into tomorrow, at least briefly. We suspect he'll hop around until he feels safe enough to settle somewhere while he plans his next move. At least we seem to have thrown him off course for a while. But mad as he is, he is just as clever. So we can't just sit by and wait. No doubt he's desperate now and will return with a vengeance."

"He's paranoid, too," Flynn said. "And all these things make for a dangerous combination, especially if he thinks he's backed into a corner."

Ben, still confused by it all, asked, "But why me? What does he think I have that he doesn't already possess? If he's that smart, he'd be well on his way to his time-travel goal."

Dave stood up and said, "Well, then let's start looking. There has to be something here that we can find. And maybe once we find it, we can wrap this thing up."

Everyone mumbled in agreement, and Wilber asked, "What are we looking for?"

Flynn, looking seductively at Jack, said, "You'll know when you find it, then you can stop looking."

With that comment, Jack blushed for only the third time in his life.

CHAPTER 12

Ben took charge of assigning members of the group to certain areas of the house, with the request that they not damage anything or tear through personal items with reckless abandon. Aunt Louise and Olivia would search the bedrooms and baths, while Wilber and Merrit were assigned the kitchen, laundry area, and outside areas, including the boats. Ben took the garage, while Jack and Dave took any other rooms not already designated.

Ben went into the garage and, looking at the boxes of his personal items that had arrived from Germany, decided he would go through them first. He knew it would be difficult, as it was a reminder of a place he had to reluctantly leave behind. Also, the memories the boxes contained, especially those things Allie had given him during their time together, would be difficult to look at. Things they shared were in there, too, and had special meaning to him. In spite of that, he began opening boxes and examining every item he touched. With no idea what to look for, he believed this was going to be an impossible endeavor, but if it would help the cause, he would do his best.

After laying almost everything on the workbench, he remembered the file he had discovered in the safe. Retrieving it, he called out for Flynn and Ian to come take a look.

Stepping into the garage, Ian took the folder and examined each page. "Good stuff, but not what we're looking for. We already had this," he said as he handed the file back to Ben. "But you're on the right track, sir. Keep looking."

As Ian and Flynn left to go about their search, Dave went in. "Any luck?" he asked. "Thought maybe you had something."

"No," Ben replied. "They already knew about the stuff I found, so there has to be something else."

"Sure have a lot of pictures here," Dave said as he shuffled through the box of photographs Ben had set on the bench.

With sadness in his voice, Ben said, "Yeah. Mom and Dad were always sending pictures to me. They loved to keep a photographic record of everything. Holidays, birthdays, trips, Mom's cooking. Didn't matter. If it happened, they had a picture of it."

"Hmmmm," Dave mumbled. "Ever notice anything peculiar about most of these pictures?" Ben moved to his side and said, "No, not really. Just pictures."

Dave grabbed a handful of photographs and told Ben to follow him to the living room. There, he stopped in front of the restored antique phonograph that Arthur had given his wife on their first wedding anniversary.

Holding the pictures out to Ben, Dave told him, "Look at these pictures. Look at them and tell me what they all have in common."

Ben quickly shuffled through the pictures and discovered the same thing Dave had picked up on. "Every one of them was taken in front of this phonograph. Dozens, if not a hundred, all the same. No matter the occasion, the phonograph holds a prominent spot in the picture. You think it means something?"

"Maybe,"Dave replied."Maybe not. Let's get Flynn's take on it."

Agent Flynn, accompanied by Ian, soon stood in front of the phonograph. Dave briefed her on what he had noticed, and she agreed it could have some significance. But what?

"Know anything about the record that's on here?" Dave asked.

Looking inside the cabinet that held the turntable, Ben replied, "Yeah. That's the opera *La bohème*, Mom's favorite record. Dad put it on here when he gave her the phonograph, and she swore she'd never take it off. She and Dad danced to it nearly every night."

"May I?" Dave asked as he reached for the record. Ben nodded.

Dave held the record carefully and closely to better examine it.

"Hmmm," he said. Then he said "hmmm" again. "Turn this thing on. I think I found something."

Ben reached inside the finely finished cabinet and switched on the turntable. Dave placed the record carefully onto the spinning platform and, to everyone's puzzlement, placed the stylus on a groove about three quarters of the way into the recording. Soft music emanated from the speaker then faded, followed by silence. Then, a man began to speak.

"Hi, Ben." It was his father. Somehow, he had recorded his own voice onto this record. While Ben was excited to hear his father's voice, an overwhelming sense of grief enveloped him, causing him to grow weak at his knees. A hand on his shoulder calmed him temporarily, and he glanced back to see Jim standing close to him. The voice continued.

"We figured that sooner or later you would play this record, so we wanted to pass something along to you. First, if anyone else is with you, please ask them to leave the room. What follows is for your ears only."

Ben made no attempt to fulfill that request, and no one made a move toward the closest door. "Something tragic has likely occurred. Otherwise, this would not be necessary. No matter what, my boy, you must continue on. Your mother and I are proud of you, who you have become. We know you'll follow your dreams and accomplish much. So go get 'em, son. We love you, always have. So don't fret. You are strong; guess you get that from your mother. Take care, we love you."

Ben, nearly in tears at this point, wished his mother had been recorded also, but there was only a few seconds of silence. Then his dad spoke again.

"What follows is classified information that must be secured by the person whose number I will give you. Don't write it down. It must be memorized, so play it over and over until you have it ingrained in your mind, then call when no one is around. Here is the number."

To Agent Flynn's amazement, the number he so carefully and clearly repeated was her private, secure line number.

"This person will know what to do with the information on this record, and they will give you instructions that must be followed to the letter. Meantime, safeguard it, and speak of it to no one. I know I can trust you to carry this out. I have never doubted you. Be strong, son. We don't know what lay ahead."

Nothing but silence followed for a time, then his father's voice began to relate mathematical equations, theoretical solutions to questions relating to time travel, both forward and backward, as well as instructions on how to design and implement equipment necessary to carry out experimental exercises based on the calculations he had noted. There was more, but Agent

Flynn removed the stylus and pulled the record from the turntable.

"Bingo," she said, reaching into the record storage compartment to locate the protective case.

She located the proper cover and turned to hand it to one of her agents.

Ben turned to Flynn and asked, "How? How did he?"

"Your father was an intelligent man, Ben," she replied. "He had a clandestine operation going for years to dissect the Philly Experiment and extract all its potential. It was he who developed the orb-tracking technology we use to monitor all Sterling's jumps. He also bumped up our capability to move in a similar fashion with the orbs we have. You see, he never really retired."

"I'll take that." They all turned to see Ian holding a firearm that looked like a real hand cannon.

From his vantage point, he could hit any one of them as they stood in front of the phonograph.

Flynn spoke calmly. "So another one comes out of the woodwork. You know you won't get far."

"It's worth trying. I'm the only one who knows how to make all this work. Sterling was too focused on one thing to see the bigger picture. Oh, the possibilities. I can do it. And I don't need help from anybody. Now, get the little girl over here. She goes with me."

Aunt Louise, with Olivia following close behind, had entered the room as Ben's father spoke. Now, Louise pulled her daughter closer, refusing the scientist's demand.

In the few seconds it took for everyone to grasp what was happening, Duke had already begun to carry out his plan. Like a streak of black lightning, he leapt at Ian, taking his gun hand in his powerful jaws, causing the man to release his grip on the firearm. Even as the man shrieked in pain, Flynn was barreling headfirst into the helpless scientist, taking him to the floor before the gun could even hit the floor.

The other two agents moved in quickly and soon had him secure and held tight. Duke, as if celebrating the successful takedown, trotted happily over to sit beside an astonished Ben.

Flynn, apparently unfazed by what had just happened, said to no one in particular, "Guess you just can't trust anyone these days. Don't know why I even stay in this business." She turned her attention to one of her agents and said, "Secure him, and get him out of my sight. Contact the Sergeant Major, and get a status on the vessel security operation and any information on Sterling's location. I also want a status on the teenagers and their families—where they are and if their briefings are complete. Same thing for the civilians on the ship. We need them out of there and in a safe place until this is over. Go."

Jack wasn't sure about anyone else, but he sure was taken by this woman—the way she handled herself under stress, how she recovered so quickly and immediately took charge. Yeah, he looked forward to getting to know her better. He still wasn't so certain, however, if he should be scared of her or not, but he was eager to find out.

"Well, now we have to come up with something, and I suspect we'll have to do it soon. No telling what Sterling might have hatched up by now," she stated, looking at Jim, Dave, and Jack as if they had the answer.

Dave replied, "We put him in a box."

"Explain," Flynn said.

Dave answered, "We keep slowly turning the power down, reducing the distance he can move, as well as the size of his 'tomorrow' bubble. In time, he won't even be able to move across the room, let alone take anything or anybody with him."

Flynn smiled slightly and said, "That just might work. You want in on it? I seem to be losing my science and technology personnel lately."

"Yes, ma'am. Just tell me where to report!"

Motioning to the remaining agent, she said, "Go with him. He'll take you to the Sergeant Major, where you'll be briefed by the team leader. It's all yours from there. Go."

Their world was quiet for the time being, a welcome relief after all that had transpired in the past few hours. Coffee was brewing, and Aunt Louise was busy preparing snacks for her newfound friends. As she worked, she engaged in small talk with Merrit, Wilber, and Olivia, who was fascinated with their stories of how they came to be captives on Sterling's ship.

Jack asked Flynn if she wanted to take a walk, and she gladly accepted the invitation to get some fresh air. As they excused themselves from the kitchen, they walked outside into the calm spring air. They casually walked to the dock without exchanging a word.

When they reached the end of the dock, they stopped and turned to each other at the same time. "What are you going to do when this circus is over?" Jack asked.

"There will be another circus, in another town. There always is," she replied.

"Don't you ever get a vacation?" he asked.

"Well," she said with a smile, "I do have some leave saved up. And I understand you and I have something in common."

"And what would that be?" He couldn't imagine what he might have in common with such a woman.

"I have a Harley in my garage too. And it's just sitting there, gathering dust. Been a while since I felt the wind in my hair," she said playfully. She chuckled at the look on his face.

"Sounds like you could use a road trip. That always clears the mind." He couldn't believe he was saying this to her and felt genuinely embarrassed about it.

"It's a date then" was all she said as they stood side by side, looking out over the still water of the creek, soon holding each other's hand in the dark.

*****

Ben, who had been sitting alone in the living room, entered the kitchen and sat on a side chair, Duke on the floor beside him. Looking at Louise and then at Olivia, he said to them both, "I'm so sorry you two got tangled up in this mess. Everything happened so fast I couldn't keep up. I would have done anything to keep you out of it."

Louise turned to him and said, "We know, Ben. This was a wild, fast ride for all of us. But it seems it is working out. What about you, dear? You've been through a lot these past couple weeks, especially the past day or so. You need a break too."

She was right, Ben thought. He hadn't had time to even think about Allie lately. And now that there might be some sense of normal coming their way, maybe he could figure out something, a way to get to her. He was exhausted now and could barely tell what day of the week it was. Maybe after a day or two of rest, he could come up with something.

For now, a good cup of coffee in familiar surroundings was welcome enough. Ben did kind of feel like the odd man out, though. Jim and Olivia grew closer every day, Jack and Agent Flynn seemed to be getting closer to each other, Aunt Louise was content to fuss over Olivia and Ben, and Dave, well, he had the orbs to play with. Ben, meanwhile, had lost his parents and the only girl he ever loved, not to mention his career, all in a matter of days. In spite of that, he was happy for his friends and wished nothing but the best for them.

Days passed, with Agent Flynn setting up her command center in Ben's garage. It was only a command center because she spent all her time there with Jack. She had arranged for her bike to be taken there, and Jack was going over it, bolt by bolt, to make sure it was up for the road trip they had planned. Anyone who needed to get in touch with her knew where to find her, and it was the agents she worked with that gave the garage its official name. Neither she nor Jack minded the joke, as long as they were together.

*****

In a marsh on the eastern side of Bloodsworth Island, a frustrated and angry man found himself knee-deep in mud. Mosquitoes were biting every inch of exposed skin, while others buzzed around him, waiting their turn to suck out any blood that might be left in his veins.

"Must be low tide," he mumbled to himself as he fought to ignore the stench of the mud and dead-sea-life salad that surrounded him. He tried to kick the orb that had taken him there, but both feet were held fast below him. He figured something must have happened to the power supply back at the ship after that intrusion a few days ago. Since then, he discovered he couldn't move as far as before and not as far into tomorrow as he would have liked. *What a mess*, he thought. *When I get my hands on them.*

The sound of someone clearing their throat startled him. As he looked up across the marsh grass and cattails, he saw not one, but at least a dozen heavily armed men staring at him. Some were trying to stifle a laugh, while most wore stern faces. One of the men standing behind the others spoke into his wrist, "We've got him."

It wasn't long before Dave called with the news. His plan had worked, and they were able to catch Mr. Sterling. Just as Dave had figured, the power for his orb was so low he couldn't move ahead more than a minute and no farther than a couple of yards by the time they found him. A miscalculation had put him in a marsh not far from the shore of the bay. A special operations team was there to fish him out. Tired, hungry, and terribly disheveled, he offered no resistance as they took him away. Though the news was certainly good, there were other, smaller-level culprits to find and put away, but it was enough to cause celebration among those present at the Dawson house.

The nightmare was over, and the missing and wounded were returned to their families. For those needing medical attention, such as the disfigured watermen, highly trained medical personnel, the best in the world, were assembled and began the arduous task of restoring their bodies to as close to normal as possible.

After some years of quiet rest, Sterling's ship once again became a target at which Navy planes could discharge their powerful weapons. This time, target practice didn't cease until there was little visible above the waterline.

In time, the events they had endured would be a faint memory. Not a particularly good memory, but faint nevertheless. They were strong, after all, and could now face nearly any challenge put before them. Gone were the black sedans, the mysterious, silent boats that once turned up on the creek near Ben's house, and people who appeared then vanished like smoke on a windy day.

Spring was making its presence known on Maryland's eastern shore, and life went back to normal. Tomorrow could wait until they were ready to step into it. And that was how it was meant to be. As Aunt Louise so wisely put it, "You can't force those things that can't be. Things will happen on their own, and when they happen, you'll know it, and you'll be ready." Indeed.

EPILOGUE

....

Ben sat on the dock, listening to the radio, the warm spring sun high in the afternoon sky. Duke lay beside him, twitching his nose on occasion, maybe catching a scent he found interesting. No plan Ben could think of was practical enough to bring him and Allie back together. He wondered if she thought he had simply abandoned her, that he chose to just write off their relationship. She couldn't think that, even though he had given her no reason to think any differently. Why hadn't he told her how he felt about her when he had the chance? There was always tomorrow, and that didn't work out too well.

Now, he found sleep elusive, lying awake nearly every night, afraid to dream yet wishing he could. That was the only way he could see her, even though it left him sad and exhausted each time she came to him in his sleep. Aunt Louise had tried many times to console him, but he resisted, maybe to punish himself for allowing Allie to slip from his life. He tried to tell himself that maybe she felt different about their relationship, that she had likely found someone new and completely forgot about him. Of course, that didn't help much either.

As he lay there feeling sorry for himself, a sedan pulled into the driveway. This one wasn't black like the ones they used to see, but Army green. As he got up to go see who it might be, a familiar figure got out of the passenger side. It was Sergeant Major Hammer.

"Hello again, Ben," he said, holding out his hand to greet Ben with a handshake. "How you been doing, young man?"

"Okay, I guess. Good to see you, Sergeant Major." Ben shook his hand and motioned for him to have a seat with him on the dock.

"I only have a few minutes, Sergeant. I've got some good news for you."

The fact that he was just addressed as Sergeant didn't escape Ben, and he couldn't keep from smiling. Holding out a folder for Ben to take, the Sergeant Major continued, "These are your orders. You'll report to Fort Hood next month, at your current rank. After your processing, you'll report to the Warrant Officer Selection Board. The dates and instructions are attached. Any questions?"

Ben couldn't contain himself. "No, Sergeant Major, thank you. But how?"

"You should have never been discharged in the first place. All things considered, it was pretty easy to get you back in uniform. Maybe we'll meet again. Gotta go. Good luck, Sergeant Dawson."

With that, the Sergeant Major turned and walked back toward the waiting sedan. Just as he was about to open the door, he turned back and approached Ben.

"I almost forgot," he said as he gave Ben an envelope. "You'll want this too. See you later, young man."

He went to the sedan, got in, and was gone.

As he walked to the house to tell Aunt Louise the good news, he opened the envelope to see what it contained. It was a single sheet of paper with only a name and address typed on it. When he read it, he took off running, making it difficult for even Duke to keep up.

He burst through the kitchen door, yelling, "Aunt Louise, Aunt Louise, I've got to pack. I've got to go!"

Shocked by his entrance, she asked, "What on earth are you so fired up about? What do you mean pack? Go where?"

"The Army!" he exclaimed. "I'm going back. And Allie. I've gotta go. It's a long way to Albuquerque!"

*****

On a winding mountain highway in North Carolina, Jack and Pepsy leaned their respective motorcycles through the gentle curves, powering up and down the rolling hills, and laughed as they put mile after mile of country behind them. This was what they had been waiting for: just the two of them riding toward the horizon, no destination in mind, stopping when they felt like it, riding on if they didn't. Now and then, they would exchange glances, maybe to see if this was real. Life was good.

Rounding a curve in the highway, Jack noticed a sedan gaining speed and approaching quickly from behind. Pepsy noticed it, too, just as it pulled up beside them and motioned for them to stop. Jack had hoped they had seen the last of those sedans, especially when they were black like this one.

After they had stopped on the side of the highway, Pepsy got off her bike and met the man who had come from the passenger side of the car. Though Jack was unable to hear what they were saying as passing cars drowned out their conversation, he could tell that the man was serious and Pepsy wasn't happy. *I guess this is her next circus already*, Jack thought. And they had barely started their trip.

Soon the car pulled away, and Pepsy mounted her bike. She turned to Jack and, as she started her bike, said, "We've got to go back. Sterling has disappeared."

Now riding north, Pepsy realized that the operation Sterling was conducting went far deeper than she had anticipated. She figured he must have allies all through the government, infesting several agencies and divisions. It was clear that cleaning this up was going to take a while, and road trips with the man she had come to feel very strongly about would have to wait. She would have to tell him sooner or later, but she would do it tomorrow. There was always tomorrow.

"I don't know why I ever stay in this business," she said to the wind.

Printed in the USA
CPSIA information can be obtained
at www.ICGtesting.com
LVHW092057230424
778232LV00003B/218